"If you take me to the auction as your date, you'll win your bet."

"It violates the spirit of it."

"It doesn't have to," Chase insisted. "Anyway, by the time I'm through with you, you'll be able to get any date you want."

She blinked. "Are you...are you Henry Higgins-ing me?"

He only had a vague knowledge of the old movie *My Fair Lady*, but he was pretty sure that was the reference. A man who took a grubby flower girl and turned her into the talk of the town.

"Yes," he said finally. "Yes, I am. Take me up on this, Anna Brown, and I will turn you into a woman."

* * *

Take Me, Cowboy is part of the Copper Ridge series from *USA TODAY* bestselling author Maisey Yates

Dear Reader,

My Copper Ridge series celebrates community, family, love and, of course, hot cowboys, and I'm so thrilled to bring new stories set in this vibrant Oregon town to Harlequin Desire.

One of my favorite things to write is a friends-to-lovers romance. I love that moment when the hero and heroine suddenly see each other in a different light. And I love it when the resistance gives way and they just can't fight their attraction anymore. That's why I'm excited to introduce Chase, my playboy cowboy, and Anna, the one woman who never tried to lasso his heart.

Chase and Anna have been good friends for fifteen years. Even though Anna has always had the hots for Chase, she's never acted on her feelings for fear of damaging their friendship. But a bet, a fake date and some late-night flirting lessons change everything, and once they've crossed the line, it won't be easy to go back.

If you enjoy Chase and Anna and your time in Copper Ridge, I hope you'll check out more stories set there. In May, you can find my brand-new release, *One Night Charmer*, coming out with HQN Books. It features Ace, the ridiculously sexy bar owner, whom you'll meet in this story. Then Chase's brother Sam will return this November in *Hold Me, Cowboy*. Meanwhile, if you'd like to start at the beginning of the series, *Shoulda Been a Cowboy* is available now.

Happy reading!

Maisey

TAKE ME, COWBOY

MAISEY YATES

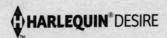
HARLEQUIN®DESIRE

Recycling programs
for this product may
not exist in your area.

ISBN-13: 978-0-373-73450-4

Take Me, Cowboy

Copyright © 2016 by Maisey Yates

This edition published by arrangement with Harlequin Books S.A.

For questions and comments about the quality of this book, please contact us at CustomerService@Harlequin.com.

® and TM are trademarks of Harlequin Enterprises Limited or its corporate affiliates. Trademarks indicated with ® are registered in the United States Patent and Trademark Office, the Canadian Intellectual Property Office and in other countries.

Printed in U.S.A.

Maisey Yates is a *USA TODAY* bestselling author of more than thirty romance novels. She has a coffee habit she has no interest in kicking and a slight Pinterest addiction. She lives with her husband and children in the Pacific Northwest. When Maisey isn't writing she can be found singing in the grocery store, shopping for shoes online and probably not doing dishes. Check out her website, maiseyyates.com.

Books by Maisey Yates

HARLEQUIN DESIRE

Copper Ridge

Take Me, Cowboy

HQN BOOKS

Copper Ridge

Shoulda Been a Cowboy
Part Time Cowboy
Brokedown Cowboy
Bad News Cowboy
A Copper Ridge Christmas
One Night Charmer

HARLEQUIN PRESENTS

Bound to the Warrior King
His Diamond of Convenience
To Defy a Sheikh
One Night to Risk it All
Forged in the Desert Heat
His Ring Is Not Enough
The Couple Who Fooled the World
A Game of Vows

Visit her Author Profile page on Harlequin.com, or maiseyyates.com, for more titles!

To Nicole Helm, for your friendship, profane texts and love of farm animals in sweaters. My life would be boring without you.

One

When Anna Brown walked into Ace's bar, she was contemplating whether or not she could get away with murdering her older brothers.

That's really nice that the invitation includes a plus one. You know you can't bring your socket wrench.

She wanted to punch Daniel in his smug face for that one. She had been flattered when she'd received her invitation to the community charity event that the West family hosted every year. A lot less so when Daniel and Mark had gotten ahold of it and decided it was the funniest thing in the world to imagine her trying to get a date to the coveted fund-raiser.

Because apparently the idea of her having a date at all was the pinnacle of comedic genius.

I can get a date, jackasses.

You want to make a bet?

Sure. It's your money.

That exchange had seemed both enraging and empowering about an hour ago. Now she was feeling both humiliated and a little bit uncertain. The fact that she had bet on her dating prowess was...well, embarrassing didn't even begin to describe it. But on top of that, she was a little concerned that she had no prowess to speak of.

It had been longer than she wanted to admit since she'd actually had a date. In fact, it was entirely possible that she had never technically been on one. That quick roll in the literal hay with Corbin Martin hadn't exactly been a date per se.

And it hadn't led to anything, either. Since she had done a wonderful job of smashing his ego with a hammer the next day at school when she'd told her best friend, Chase, about Corbin's...limitations.

Yeah, her sexual debut had also been the final curtain.

But if men weren't such whiny babies, maybe that wouldn't have been the case. Also, maybe if Corbin had been able to prove to her that sex was worth the trouble, she would view it differently.

But he hadn't. So she didn't.

And now she needed a date.

She stalked across the room, heading toward the table that she and Chase, and often his brother, Sam, occupied on Friday nights. The lighting was dim, so she knew someone was sitting there but couldn't make out which Mc-Cormack brother it was.

She hoped it was Chase. Because as long as she'd known Sam, she still had a hard time making conversation with him.

Talking wasn't really his thing.

She moved closer, and the man at the table tilted his head up. Sam. Dammit. Drinking a beer and looking grumpy, which was pretty much par for the course with him. But Chase was nowhere to be seen.

"Hi," she said, plopping down in the chair beside him. "Bad day?"

"A day."

"Right." At least when it came to Sam, she knew the difficult-conversation thing had nothing to do with her. That was all him.

She tapped the top of her knee, looking around the bar, trying to decide if she was going to get up and order a drink or wait for someone to come to the table. She allowed her gaze to drift across the bar, and her attention was caught by the figure of a man in the corner, black cowboy hat on his head, his face shrouded by the dim light. A woman was standing in front of him looking up at his face like he was her every birthday wish come true.

For a moment the sight of the man standing there struck her completely dumb. Broad shoulders, broad chest, strong-looking hands. The kind of hands that made her wonder if she needed to investigate the potential fuss of sex again.

He leaned up against the wall, his forearm above his head. He said something and the little blonde he was talking to practically shimmered with excitement. Anna wondered what that was like. To be the focus of a man's attention like that. To have him look at you like a sex object instead of a drinking buddy.

For a moment she envied the woman standing there, who could absolutely get a date if she wanted one. Who would know what to wear and how to act if she were invited to a fancy gala whatever.

That woman would know what to do if the guy wanted to take her home after the date and get naked. She wouldn't be awkward and make jokes and laugh when he got naked because there were all these feelings that were so…so weird she didn't know how else to react.

With a man like that one…well, she doubted she would laugh. He would be all lean muscle and wicked smiles. He would look at her and she would… Okay, even in fantasy she didn't know. But she felt hot. Very, very hot.

But in a flash, that hot feeling turned into utter horror. Because the man shifted, pushing his hat back on his head and angling slightly toward Anna, a light from above catching his angular features and illuminating his face. He changed then, from a fantasy to flesh and blood. And she realized exactly who she had just been checking out.

Chase McCormack. Her best friend in the entire world. The man she had spent years training herself to never, ever have feelings below the belt for.

She blinked rapidly, squeezing her hands into fists and trying to calm the fluttering in her stomach. "I'm going to get a drink," she said, looking at Sam. *And talk to Ace about the damn lighting in here.* "Did you want something?"

He lifted his brow, and his bottle of beer. "I'm covered."

Her heart was still pounding a little heavier than usual when she reached the bar and signaled Ace, the establishment's owner, to ask for whatever pale ale he had on tap.

And her heart stopped altogether when she heard a deep voice from behind her.

"Why don't you make that two."

She whisked around and came face-to-chest with Chase. A man whose presence should be commonplace, and usually was. She was just in a weird place, thanks to high-pressure invitations and idiot brothers.

"Pale ale," she said, taking a step back and looking up at his face. A face that should also be commonplace. But it was just so very symmetrical. Square jaw, straight nose, strong brows and dark eyes that were so direct they bordered on obscene. Like they were looking straight through your clothes or something. Not that he would ever want to look through hers. Not that she would want him to. She was too smart for that.

"That's kind of an unusual order for you," she continued,

more to remind herself of who he was than to actually make commentary on his beverage choices. To remind herself that she knew him better than she knew herself. To do whatever she could to put that temporary moment of insanity when she'd spotted him in the corner out of her mind.

"I'm feeling adventurous," he said, lifting one corner of his mouth, the lopsided grin disrupting the symmetry she had been admiring earlier and somehow making him look all the more compelling for it.

"Come on, McCormack. Adventurous is bungee jumping from Multnomah Falls. Adventurous is not trying a new beer."

"Says the expert in adventure?"

"I'm an expert in a couple of things. Beer and motor oil being at the top of the list."

"Then I won't challenge you."

"Probably for the best. I'm feeling a little bit bloodthirsty tonight." She pressed her hands onto the bar top and leaned forward, watching as Ace went to get their drinks. "So. Why aren't you still talking to short, blonde and stacked over there?"

He chuckled and it settled oddly inside her chest, rattling around before skittering down her spine. "Not really all that interested."

"You seemed interested to me."

"Well," he said, "I'm not."

"That's inconsistent," she said.

"Okay, I'll bite," he said, regarding her a little more closely than she would like. "Why are you in the mood to cause death and dismemberment?"

"Do I seem that feral?"

"Completely. Why?"

"The same reason I usually am," she said.

"Your brothers."

"You're fast, I like that."

Ace returned to their end of the bar and passed two pints toward them. "Do you want to open a tab?"

"Sure," she said. "On him." She gestured to Chase.

Ace smiled in return. "You look nice tonight, Anna."

"I look…the same as I always do," she said, glancing down at her worn gray T-shirt and no-fuss jeans.

He winked. "Exactly."

She looked up at Chase, who was staring at the bartender, his expression unreadable. Then she looked back at Ace.

Ace was pretty hot, really. In that bearded, flannel-wearing way. Lumbersexual, or so she had overheard some college girls saying the other night as they giggled over him. Maybe *he* would want to be her date. Of course, easy compliments and charm aside, he also had his pick of any woman who turned up in his bar. And Anna was never anyone's pick.

She let go of her fleeting Ace fantasy pretty quickly.

Chase grabbed the beer from the counter and handed one to her. She was careful not to let their fingers brush as she took it from him. That type of avoidance was second nature to her. Hazards of spending the years since adolescence feeling electricity when Chase got too close, and pretending she didn't.

"We should go back and sit with Sam," she suggested. "He looks lonely."

Chase laughed. "You and I both know he's no such thing. I think he would rather sit there alone."

"Well, if he wants to be alone, then he can stay at home and drink."

"He probably would if I didn't force him to come out. But if I didn't do that, he would fuse to the furniture and then I would have all of that to deal with."

They walked back over to the table, and gradually, her

heart rate returned to normal. She was relieved that the initial weirdness she had felt upon his arrival was receding.

"Hi, Sam," Chase said, taking his seat beside his brother. Sam grunted in response. "We were just talking about the hazards of you turning into a hermit."

"Am I not a convincing hermit already?" he asked. "Do I need to make my disdain for mankind a little less subtle?"

"That might help," Chase said.

"I might just go play a game of darts instead. I'll catch up with you in a minute." Sam took a long drink of his beer and stood, leaving the bottle on the table as he made his way over to the dartboard across the bar.

Silence settled between Chase and herself. Why was this suddenly weird? Why was Anna suddenly conscious of the way his throat moved when he swallowed a sip of beer, of the shift in his forearms as he set the bottle back down on the table? Of just how masculine a sound he made when he cleared his throat?

She was suddenly even conscious of the way he breathed.

She leaned back in her chair, lifting her beer to her lips and surveying the scene around them.

It was Friday night, so most of the town of Copper Ridge, Oregon, was hanging out, drowning the last vestiges of the workweek in booze. It was not the end of the workweek for Anna. Farmers and ranchers didn't take time off, so neither did she. She had to be on hand to make repairs when necessary, especially right now, since she was just getting her own garage off the ground.

She'd just recently quit her job at Jake's in order to open her own shop specializing in heavy equipment, which really was how she found herself in the position she was in right now. Invited to the charity gala thing and embroiled in a bet on whether or not she could get a date.

"So why exactly do you want to kill your brothers today?" Chase asked, startling her out of her thoughts.

"Various reasons." She didn't know why, but something stopped her from wanting to tell him exactly what was going on. Maybe because it was humiliating. Yes, it was definitely humiliating.

"Sure. But that's every day. Why specifically do you want to kill them today?"

She took a deep breath, keeping her eyes fixed on the fishing boat that was mounted to the wall opposite her, and very determinedly not looking at Chase. "Because. They bet that I couldn't get a date to this thing I'm invited to and I bet them that I could." She thought about the woman he'd been talking to a moment ago. A woman so different from herself they might as well be different species. "And right about now I'm afraid they're right."

Chase was doing his best to process his best friend's statement. It was difficult, though. Daniel and Mark had solid asshole tendencies when it came to Anna—that much he knew—but this was pretty low even for them.

He studied Anna's profile, her dark hair pulled back into a braid, her gray T-shirt that was streaked with oil. He watched as she raised her bottle of beer to her lips. She had oil on her hands, too. Beneath her fingernails. Anna wasn't the kind of girl who attracted a lot of male attention. But he kind of figured that was her choice.

She wasn't conventionally beautiful. Mostly because of the motor oil. But that didn't mean that getting a date should be impossible for her.

"Why don't you think you can get a date?"

She snorted, looking over at him, one dark brow raised. "Um." She waved a hand up and down, indicating her body. "Because of all of this."

He took a moment to look at *all of that*. Really look. Like he was a man and she was a woman. Which they were, but not in a conventional sense. Not to each other.

He'd looked at her almost every day for the past fifteen years, so it was difficult to imagine seeing her for the first time. But just then, he tried.

She had a nice nose. And her lips were full, nicely shaped, her top lip a little fuller than her bottom lip, which was unique and sort of…not sexy, because it was Anna. But interesting.

"A little elbow grease and that cleans right off," he said. "Anyway, men are pretty simple."

She frowned. "What does that mean?"

"Exactly what it sounds like. You don't have to do much to get male attention if you want it. Give a guy what he's after…"

"Okay, that's just insulting. You're saying that I can get a guy because men just want to get laid? So it doesn't matter if I'm a wrench-toting troll?"

"You are not a wrench-toting troll. You're a wrench-toting woman who could easily bludgeon me to death, and I am aware of that. Which means I need to choose my next words a little more carefully."

Those full lips thinned into a dangerous line, her green eyes glittering dangerously. "Why don't you do that, Chase."

He cleared his throat. "I'm just saying, if you want a date, you can get one."

"By unzipping my coveralls down to my belly button?"

He tipped his beer bottle back, taking a larger swallow than he intended to, coughing as it went down wrong. He did not need to picture the visual she had just handed to him. But he was a man, so he did.

It was damned unsettling. His best friend, bare beneath a pair of coveralls unfastened so that a very generous wedge of skin was revealed all the way down…

And he was done with that. He didn't think of Anna that way. Not at all. They'd been friends since they were freshmen in high school and he'd navigated teenage boy hormones without lingering too long on thoughts of her breasts.

He was thirty years old, and he could have sex whenever he damn well pleased. Breasts were no longer mysterious to him. He wasn't going to go pondering the mysteries of *her* breasts now.

"It couldn't hurt, Anna," he said, his words containing a little more bite than he would like them to. But he was unsettled.

"Okay, I'll keep that in mind. But barring that, do you have any other suggestions? Because I think I'm going to be expected to wear something fancy, and I don't own anything fancy. And it's obvious that Mark and Daniel think I suck at being a girl."

"That's not true. And anyway, why do you care what they—or anyone else—think?"

"Because. I've got this new business…"

"And anyone who brings their heavy equipment to you for a tune-up won't care whether or not you can walk in high heels."

"But I don't want to show up at these things looking…" She sighed. "Chase, the bottom line is I've spent a long time not fitting in. And people here are nice to me. I mean, now that I'm not in school. People in school sucked. But I get that I don't fit. And I'm tired of it. Honestly, I wouldn't care about my brothers if there wasn't so much…truth to the teasing."

"They do suck. They're awful. So why does it matter what they think?"

"Because," she said. "It just does. I'm that poor Anna Brown with no mom to teach her the right way to do things and I'm just…tired of it. I don't want to be poor Anna Brown. I want to be Anna Brown, heavy equipment mechanic who can wear coveralls and walk in heels."

"Not at the same time, I wouldn't think."

She shot him a deadly glare. "I don't fail," she said, her eyes glinting in the dim bar light. "I won't fail at this."

"You're not in remote danger of failing. Now, what's the mystery event that has you thinking about high heels?" he asked.

Copper Ridge wasn't exactly a societal epicenter. Nestled between the evergreen mountains and a steel-gray sea on the Oregon Coast, there were probably more deer than people in the small town. There were only so many events in existence. And there was a good chance she was making a mountain out of a small-town molehill, and none of it would be that big of a deal.

"That charity thing that the West family has every year," she mumbled. "Gala Under the Stars or whatever."

The West family's annual fund-raising event for schools. It was a weekend event, with the town's top earners coming to a small black-tie get-together on the West property.

The McCormacks had been founding members of the community of Copper Ridge back in the 1800s. Their forge had been used by everyone in town and in the neighboring communities. But as the economy had changed, so had the success of the business.

They'd been hanging on by their fingernails when Chase's parents had been killed in an accident when he was in high school. They'd still gotten an invitation to the gala. But Chase had thrown it on top of the never-ending pile of mail and bills that he couldn't bring himself to look through and forgotten about it.

Until some woman—probably an assistant to the West family—had called him one year when he hadn't bothered to RSVP. He had been…well, he'd been less than polite.

Dealing with a damned crisis here, so sorry I can't go to your party.

Unsurprisingly, he hadn't gotten any invitations after that. And he hadn't really thought much about it since.

Until now.

He and Sam had managed to keep the operation and properties afloat, but he wanted more. He needed it.

The ranch had animals, but that wasn't the source of their income. The forge was the heart of the ranch, where they did premium custom metal- and leatherwork. On top of that, there were outbuildings on the property they rented out—including the shop they leased to Anna. They had built things back up since their parents had died, but it still wasn't enough, not to Chase.

He had promised his father he would take an interest in the family legacy. That he would build for the McCormacks, not just for himself. Chase had promised he wouldn't let his dad down. He'd had to make those promises at a grave site because before the accident he'd been a hotheaded jackass who'd thought he was too big for the family legacy.

But even if his father never knew, Chase had sworn it. And so he'd see it done.

In order to expand McCormack Iron Works, the heart and soul of their ranch, to bring it back to what it had been, they needed interest. Investments.

Chase had always had a good business mind, and early on he'd imagined he would go to school away from Copper Ridge. Get a degree. Find work in the city. Then everything had changed. Then it hadn't been about Chase McCormack anymore. It had been about the McCormack legacy.

School had become out of the question. Leaving had been out of the question. But now he saw where he and Sam were failing, and he could see how to turn the tide.

He'd spent a lot of late nights figuring out exactly how to expand as the demand for handmade items had gone down. Finding ways to convince people that highly customized iron details for homes and businesses, and handmade leather bridles and saddles, were worth paying more for.

Finding ways to push harder, to innovate and modernize while staying true to the family name. While actively butting up against Sam and his refusal to go out and make that happen. Sam, who was so talented he didn't have to pound horseshoe nails if he didn't want to. Sam, who could forget gates and scrollwork on staircases and be selling his artwork for a small fortune. Sam, who resisted change like it was the black plague.

He would kill for an invitation to the Wests' event. Well, not kill. But possibly engage in nefarious activities or the trading of sexual favors. And Anna had an invitation.

"You get to bring a date?" he asked.

"That's what I've been saying," she said. "Of course, it all depends on whether or not I can actually acquire one."

Anna needed a date; he wanted to have a chance to talk to Nathan West. In the grand tradition of their friendship, they both filled the gaps in each other's lives. This was— in his opinion—perfect.

"I'll be your date," he said.

She snorted. "Yeah, right. Daniel and Mark will never believe that."

She had a point. The two of them had been friends forever. And with a bet on the table her brothers would never believe that he had suddenly decided to go out with her because his feelings had randomly changed.

"Okay. Maybe that's true." That frown was back. "Not because there's something wrong with you," he continued, trying to dig himself out of the pit he'd just thrown himself into, "but because it's a little too convenient."

"Okay, that's better."

"But what if we made it clear that things had changed between us?"

"What do you mean?"

"I mean…what if…we built up the change? Showed people that our relationship was evolving."

She gave him a fierce side-eye. "I'm not your type." He thought back to the blonde he'd been talking to only twenty minutes earlier. Tight dress cut up to the tops of her thighs, long, wavy hair and the kind of smile that invited you right on in. Curves that had probably wrecked more men than windy Highway 101. She was his type.

And she wasn't Anna. Barefaced, scowling with a figure that was slightly more…subtle. He cleared his throat. "You could be. A little less grease, a little more lipstick."

Her top lip curled. "So the ninth circle of hell basically."

"What were you planning on wearing to the fund-raiser?"

She shifted uncomfortably in her seat. "I have black jeans. But…I mean, I guess I could go to the mall in Tolowa and get a dress."

"That isn't going to work."

"Why not?"

"What kind of dress would you buy?" he asked.

"Something floral? Kind of…down to the knee?"

He pinched the bridge of his nose. "You're not Scarlett O'Hara," he said, knowing that with her love of old movies, Anna would appreciate the reference. "You aren't going dressed in the drapes."

Anna scowled. "Why the hell do you know so much about women's clothes?"

"Because I spend a lot of time taking them off my dates."

That shut her up. Her pale cheeks flamed and she looked away from him, and that response stirred…well, it stirred something in his gut he wished would go the hell away.

"Why do *you* want to go anyway?" she asked, still not looking at him.

"I want to talk to Nathan West and the other businessmen there about investment opportunities. I want to prove that Sam and I are the kind of people that can move in their circles. The kind of people they want to do business with."

"And you have to put on a suit and hobnob at a gala to do that?"

"The fact is, I don't get chances like this very often, Anna. I didn't get an invitation. And I need one. Plus, if you take me, you'll win your bet."

"Unless Dan and Mark tell me you don't count."

"Loophole. If they never said you couldn't recruit a date, you're fine."

"It violates the spirit of the bet."

"It doesn't have to," he insisted. "Anyway, by the time I'm through with you, you'll be able to get any date you want."

She blinked. "Are you… Are you Henry Higgins-ing me?"

He had only a vague knowledge of the old movie *My Fair Lady*, but he was pretty sure that was the reference. A man who took a grubby flower girl and turned her into the talk of the town. "Yes," he said thoughtfully. "Yes, I am. Take me up on this, Anna Brown, and I will turn you into a woman."

Two

Anna just about laughed herself off her chair. "You're going to make me a...a...a woman?"

"Why is that funny?"

"What about it *isn't* funny?"

"I'm offering to help you."

"You're offering to help me be something that I am by birth. I mean, Chase, I get that women are kind of your thing, but that's pretty arrogant. Even with all things considered."

"Okay, obviously I'm not going to make you a woman." Something about the way he said the phrase this time hit her in an entirely different way. Made her think about *other* applications that phrase occasionally had. Things she needed to never, ever, ever, ever think about in connection with Chase.

If she valued her sanity and their friendship.

She cleared her throat, suddenly aware that it was dry and scratchy. "Obviously."

"I just meant that you need help getting a date, and I need

to go to this party. And you said that you were concerned about your appearance in the community."

"Right." He wasn't wrong. The thing was, she knew that whether or not she could blend in at an event like this didn't matter at all to how well her business did. Nobody cared if their mechanic knew which shade of lipstick she should wear. But that wasn't the point.

She—her family collectively—was the town charity case. Living on the edge of the community in a run-down house, raised by a single father who was in over his head, who spent his days at the mill. Her older brothers had been in charge of taking care of her, and they had done so. But, of course, they were also older brothers. Which meant they had tormented her while feeding and clothing her. Anyway, she didn't exactly blame them.

It wasn't like the two of them had wanted to raise a sister when they would rather be out raising hell.

Especially a sister who was committed to driving them crazy.

She loved her brothers. But that didn't mean they always had an easy relationship. It didn't mean they didn't hurt her by accident when they teased her about things. She acted invulnerable, so they assumed that she was.

But now, beneath her coveralls and engine grease, she was starting to feel a little bit battered. It was difficult to walk around with a *screw you* attitude barely covering a raw wound. Because eventually that shield started to wear down. Especially when people were used to being able to lob pretty intense rocks at that shield.

That was her life. It was either pity or a kind of merciless camaraderie that had no softness to it. Her dad, her brothers, all the guy friends she had…

And she couldn't really blame them. She had never behaved in a way that would demonstrate she needed any softness. In fact, a few months ago, a few weeks ago even, the idea would have been unthinkable to her.

But there was something about this invitation. Something about imagining herself in yet another situation where she was forced to deflect good-natured comments about her appearance, about the fact that she was more like a guy than the roughest cowboys in town. Yeah, there was something about that thought that had made her want to curl into a ball and never unfurl.

Then, even if it was unintentional, her brothers had piled on. It had hurt her feelings. Which meant she had reacted in anger, naturally. So now she had a bet. A bet, and her best friend looking at her with laser focus after having just promised he would make her a woman.

"Why do you care?" He was pressing, and she wanted to hit him now.

Which kind of summed up why she was in this position in the first place.

She swallowed hard. "Maybe I just want to surprise people. Isn't that enough?"

"You came from nothing. You started your own business with no support from your father. You're a female mechanic. I would say that you're surprising as hell."

"Well, I want to add another dimension to that. Okay?"

"Okay," he said. "Multidimensional Anna. That seems like a good idea to me."

"Where do we start?"

"With you not falling off your chair laughing at me because I've offered to make you a woman."

A giggle rose in her throat again. Hysteria. She was verging on hysteria. Because this was uncomfortable and sincere. She hated both of those things. "I'm sorry. I can't. You can't say that to me and expect me not to choke."

He looked at her again, his dark eyes intense. "Is it a problem, Anna? The idea that I might make you a woman."

He purposefully made his voice deeper. Purposefully added a kind of provocative inflection to the words. She knew he was kidding. Still, it made her chest tighten. Made her heart flutter a little bit.

Wow. How *annoying*. She hadn't had a relapse of Chase Underpants Feelings this bad in a long time.

Apparently she still hadn't recovered from her earlier bit of mistaken identity. She really needed to recover. And he needed to stop being…Chase. If at all possible.

"Is it a problem for *you*?" she asked.

"What?"

"The idea that I might make you a soprano?"

He chuckled. "You probably want to hold off on threats of castration when you're at a fancy party."

"We aren't at one right now."

She was her own worst enemy. Everything that she had just been silently complaining about, she was doing right now. Throwing out barbs the moment she got uncomfortable, because it kept people from seeing what was actually happening inside of her.

Yes, but you really need to keep Chase from seeing that you fluttered internally over something he said.

Yes. Good point.

She noticed that he was looking past her now, and she followed his line of sight. He was looking at that blonde again. "Regrets, Chase?"

He winced, looking back at her. "No."

"So. I assume that to get a guy to come up and hit on me in a bar, I have to put on a dress that is essentially a red ACE bandage sprinkled with glitter?"

He hesitated. "It's more than that."

"What?"

"Well, for a start, there's not looking at a man like you want to dismember him."

She rolled her eyes. "I don't."

"You aren't exactly approachable, Anna."

"That isn't true." She liked to play darts, and hang out, and talk about sports. What wasn't approachable about that?

"I've seen men try to talk to you," Chase continued. "You shut them down pretty quick. For example—" he barreled on before she could interrupt him "—Ace Thompson paid you a compliment back at the bar."

"Ace Thompson compliments everything with boobs."

"And a couple of weeks ago there was a guy in here that tried to buy you a drink. You told him you could buy your own."

"I *can*," she said, "and he was a stranger."

"He was flirting with you."

She thought back on that night, that guy. *Damn.* He had been flirting. "Well, he should get better at it. I'm not going to reward mediocrity. If I can't tell you're flirting, you aren't doing a very good job."

"Part of the problem is you don't think male attention is being directed at you when it actually is."

She looked back over at the shimmery blonde. "Why would any male attention be directed at me when *that's* over there?"

Chase leaned in, his expression taking on a conspiratorial quality that did…things to her insides. "Here's the thing about a girl like that. She knows she looks good. She assumes that men are looking at her. She assumes that if a man talks to her, that means he wants her."

She took a breath, trying to ease the tightness in her chest. "And that's not…a turnoff?"

"No way." He smiled, a sort of lazy half smile. "Confidence is sexy."

He kind of proved that rule. The thought made her bristle.

"All right. So far with our lessons I've learned that I

should unzip my coveralls and as long as I'm confident it will be okay."

"You forgot not looking like you want to stab someone."

"Okay. Confident, nonstabby, showing my boobs."

Chase choked on his beer. "That's a good place to start," he said, setting the bottle down. "Do you want to go play darts? I want to go play darts."

"I thought we were having female lessons."

"Rain check," he said. "How about tomorrow I come by the shop and we get started. I think I'm going to need a lesson plan."

Chase hadn't exactly excelled in school, unless it was at driving his teachers to drink. So why exactly he had decided he needed a lesson plan to teach Anna how to be a woman, he didn't know.

All he knew was that somewhere around the time they started discussing her boobs last night he had become unable to process thoughts normally. He didn't like that. He didn't like it at all. He did not like the fact that he had been forced to consider her breasts more than once in a single hour. He did not like the fact that he was facing down the possibility of thinking about them a few more times over the next few weeks.

But then, that was the game.

Not only was he teaching her how to blend in at a function like this, he was pretending to be her date.

So there was more than one level of hell to deal with. Perfect.

He cleared his throat, walking down the front porch of the farmhouse that he shared with his brother, making his way across the property toward the shop that Anna was renting and using as her business.

It was after five, so she should be knocking off by now. A good time for the two of them to meet.

He looked down at the piece of lined yellow paper in his hand. His lesson plan.

Then he pressed on, his boots crunching on the gravel as he made his way to the rustic wood building. He inhaled deeply, the last gasp of winter riding over the top of the spring air, mixing with the salt from the sea, giving it a crisp bite unique to Copper Ridge.

He relished this. The small moment of clarity before he dived right into the craziness that was his current situation.

Chase McCormack was many things, but he wasn't a coward. He was hardly going to get skittish over giving his best friend some seduction lessons.

He pushed the door open but didn't see Anna anywhere.

He looked around the room, and the dismembered tractors whose various parts weren't in any order that he could possibly define. Though he knew that it must make sense to Anna.

"Hello?"

"Just up here."

He turned, looked up and saw Anna leaning over what used to be a hayloft, looking down at him, a long dark braid hanging down.

"What exactly are you doing up there?"

"I stashed a tool up here, and now I need it. It's good storage. Of course, then I end up climbing the walls a little more often than I would like. Literally. Not figuratively."

"I figured you would be finished for the day by now."

"No. I have to get this tractor fixed for Connor Garrett. And it's been a bigger job than I thought." She disappeared from view for a moment. "But I would like a reputation as someone who makes miracles. So I better make miracles."

She planted her boot hard on the first rung of the ladder and began to climb down. She was covered from head to toe in motor oil and dust. Probably from crawling around in this space, and beneath tractors.

She jumped down past the last three rungs, brushing dirt off her thighs and leaving more behind, since her hands were coated, too. "You don't exactly look like a miracle," he said, looking her over.

She held up her hand, then displayed her middle finger. "Consider it a miracle that I don't punch you."

"Remember what we talked about? Not looking at a guy like you want to stab him? Much less threatening actual bodily harm."

"Hey, I don't think you would tell a woman that you actually wanted to hook up with that she didn't look like a miracle."

"Most women I want to hook up with aren't quite this disheveled. Before we start anyway."

Much to his surprise, color flooded her cheeks.

"Well," she said, her voice betraying nothing, "I'm not most women, Chase McCormack. I thought you would've known that by now."

Then she sauntered past him, wearing those ridiculous baggy coveralls, head held high like she was queen of the dust bowl.

"Oh, I'm well aware of that," he said. "That's part of the problem."

"And now it's your problem to fix."

"That's right. And I have the lesson plan. As promised."

She whipped around to face him, one dark brow lifted. "Oh, really?"

"Yes, really." He held up the lined notepaper.

"That's very professional."

"It's as professional as you're gonna get. Now, the first order of business is to plant the seed that we're more than friends."

She looked as though he had just suggested she eat a handful of bees. "Do we really need to do that?"

"Yeah, we *really* need to do that. You won't just have

a date for the charity event. You're going to have a date every so often until then."

She looked skeptical. "That seems…excessive."

"You want people to believe this. You don't want people to think I'm going because of a bet. You don't want your brothers to think for one moment that they might be right."

"Well, they're going to think it for a few moments at least."

"True. I mean, they are going to be suspicious. But we can make this look real. It isn't going to be that hard. We already hang out most weekends."

"Sure," she said, "but you go home with other girls at the end of the night."

Those words struck him down. "Yes, I guess I do."

"You won't be able to do that now," she pointed out.

"Why not?" he asked.

"Because if I were with you and you went home with another woman, I would castrate you with nothing but my car keys and a bottle of whiskey."

He had no doubt about that. "At least you'd give me some whiskey."

"Hell no. The whiskey would be for me."

"But we're not really together," he said.

"Sure, Chase, but the entire town knows that if any man were to cheat on me, I would castrate him with my car keys, because I don't take crap from anyone. So if they're going to believe that we're together, you're going to have to look like you're being faithful to me."

"That's fine." It wasn't all that fine. He didn't do celibacy. Never had. Not from the moment he'd discovered that women were God's greatest invention.

"No booty calls," she said, her tone stern.

"Wait a second. I can't even call a woman to hook up in private?"

"No. You can't. Because then *she* would know. I have

pride. I mean, right now, standing here in this garage taking lessons from you on how to conform to my own gender's beauty standards, it's definitely marginal, but I have it."

"It isn't like you really know any of the girls that I…"

"Neither do you," she said.

"This isn't about me. It's about you. Now, I got you some things. But I left them in the house. And you are going to have to…hose off before you put them on."

She blinked, her expression almost comical. "Did you buy me clothes?"

He'd taken a long lunch and gone down to Main Street, popping into one of the ridiculously expensive shops that— in his mind—were mostly for tourists, and had found her a dress he thought would work.

"Yeah, I bought you clothes. Because we both know you can't actually wear this out tonight."

"We're going out *tonight*?"

"Hell yeah. I'm taking you somewhere fancy."

"My fancy threshold is very low. If I have to go eat tiny food on a stick sometime next month, I'm going to need actual sustenance in every other meal until then."

He chuckled, trying to imagine Anna coping with miniature food. "Beaches. I'm taking you to Beaches."

She screwed up her face slightly. "We don't go there."

"No, we haven't gone there. We go to Ace's. We shoot pool, we order fried crap and we split the tab. Because we're friends. And that's what friends do. Friends don't go out to Beaches, not just the two of them. But lovers do."

She looked at him owlishly. "Right. I suppose they do."

"And when all this is finished, the entire town of Copper Ridge is going to think that we're lovers."

Three

Anna was reeling slightly by the time she walked up the front porch and into Chase's house. The entire town was going to think that they were…*lovers*. She had never had a lover. At least, she would never characterize the guy she'd slept with as a lover. He was an unfortunate incident. But fortunately, her hymen was the only casualty. Her heart had remained intact, and she was otherwise uninjured. Or pleasured.

Lovers.

That word sounded…well, like it came from some old movie or something. Which under normal circumstances she was a big fan of. In this circumstance, it just made her feel…like her insides were vibrating. She didn't like it.

Chase lived in the old family home on the property. It was a large, log cabin–style house with warm, honey-colored wood and a green metal roof designed to withstand all kinds of weather. Wrought-iron details on the porch and the door were a testament to his and Sam's craftsmanship.

There were people who would pay millions for a home like this. But Sam and Chase had made it this beautiful on their own.

Chase always kept the home admirably clean considering he was a bachelor. She imagined that the other house on the property, the smaller one inhabited by Sam, wasn't quite as well kept. But she also imagined that Sam didn't have the same amount of guests over that Chase did. And by *guests*, she meant female companions. Which he would be cut off from for the next few weeks.

Some small, mean part of her took a little bit of joy in that.

Because you don't like the idea of other women touching him. It doesn't matter how long it's been going on, or how many women there are, you still don't like it.

She sniffed, cutting off that line of thinking. She was just a crabby bitch who was enjoying the idea of him being celibate and suffering a bit. That was all.

"Okay, where are my…girlie things?"

"You aren't even going to look at them until you scrub that grease off."

"And how am I supposed to do that? Are you going to hose me off?"

He clenched his jaw. "No. You can use my shower."

She took a deep breath, trying to dispel the slight fluttering in her stomach. She had never used Chase's shower before. She assumed countless women before her had. When he brought them up here, took their clothes off for them. And probably joined them.

She wasn't going to think about that.

"Okay."

She knew where his shower was, of course. Because she had been inside his bedroom casually, countless times. It had never mattered before. Before, she had never been about to get naked.

She banished that thought as she walked up the stairs

and down the hall to his room. His room was…well, it was very well-appointed, but then again, obviously designed to house guests of the female variety. The bed was large and full of plush pillows. A soft-looking green throw was folded up at the foot of it. An overstuffed chair was in the corner, another blanket draped over the back.

She doubted the explosion of comfort and cozy was for Chase's benefit.

She tamped that thought down, continuing on through the bathroom door, then locking it for good measure. Not that he would walk in. And he was the only person in the house.

Still, she felt insecure without the lock flipped. She took a deep breath, stripped off her coveralls, then the clothes she had on beneath them, and started the shower. Speaking of things that were designed to be shared…

It was enclosed in glass, and she had a feeling that with the door open it was right in the line of sight from the bed. Inside was red tile, and a bench seat that… She wasn't even going to think what that could be used for.

She turned and looked in the mirror. She was grubby. More than grubby. She had grease all over her face, all up under her fingernails.

Thankfully, Chase had some orange-and-pumice cleaner right there on his sink. So she was able to start scrubbing at her hands while the water warmed up.

Steam filled the air and she stepped inside the shower, letting the hot spray cascade over her skin.

It was a *massaging* showerhead. A nice one. She did not have a nice massaging showerhead in her little rental house down in town. Next on her list of Ways She Was Changing Her Life would be to get her own house. With one of these.

She rolled her shoulders beneath the spray and sighed. The water droplets almost felt like fingers moving over her tight muscles. And, suddenly, it was all too easy to imagine a man standing behind her, working at her muscles with his strong hands.

She closed her eyes, letting her head fall back, her mouth going slack. She didn't even have the strength to fight the fantasy, God help her. She'd been edgy and aroused for the past twenty-four hours, no denying it. So this little moment to let herself fantasize…she just needed it.

Then she realized exactly whose hands she was picturing.

Chase's. Tall and strong behind her, his hands moving over her skin, down lower to the slight dip in her spine, just above the curve of her behind…

She grabbed hold of the sponge hanging behind her and began to drag it ferociously over her skin, only belatedly realizing that this was probably what he used to wash himself.

"He uses it to wash his balls," she said into the space. Hoping that that would disgust her. It really should disgust her.

It did not disgust her.

She put the scrubber back, taking a little shower gel and squeezing it into the palm of her hand. Okay, so she would smell like a playboy for a day. It wasn't the end of the world. She started to rub the slick soap over her flesh, ignoring the images of Chase that were trying to intrude.

She was being a crazy person. She had showered at friends' houses before, and never imagined that they were in the shower stall with her.

But ever since last night in the bar, her equilibrium had been off where Chase was concerned. Her control was being sorely tested. She was decidedly unstoked about it.

She shut the water off and got out of the shower, grabbing a towel off the rack and drying her skin with more ferocity than was strictly necessary. Almost as though she was trying to punish her wicked, wicked skin for imagining what it might be like to be touched by her best friend.

But that would be crazy.

Except she felt a little crazy.

She looked around the room. And realized that her stupid friend, who had not wanted her to touch the nice clothing he had bought her, had left her without anything to wear. She couldn't put her sweaty, grease-covered clothes back on. That would negate the entire shower.

She let out an exasperated breath, not entirely certain what she should do.

"Chase?" she called.

She didn't hear anything.

"Chase?" She raised the volume this time.

Still no answer.

"Butthead," she muttered, walking over to the door and tapping the doorknob, trying to decide what her next move was.

She was being ridiculous. Just because she was having an increase of weird, borderline sexual thoughts about him, did not mean he was having them about her. She twisted the knob, undoing the lock as she did, and opened the door a crack. "Chase!"

The door to the bedroom swung open, and Chase walked in, carrying one of those plastic bags fancy dresses were stored in and a pair of shoes.

"I don't have clothes," she hissed through the crack in the door.

"Sorry," he said, looking stricken. At least, she thought he looked stricken.

She opened the door slightly wider, extending her arm outside. "Give them to me."

He crossed the room, walking over to the bathroom door. "You're going to have to open the door wider than that."

She already felt exposed. There was nothing between them. Nothing but some air and the towel she was clutching to her naked body. Well, and most of the door. But she still felt exposed.

Still, he was not going to fit that bag through the crack.

She opened the door slightly wider, then grabbed hold of the bag in his hand and jerked it back through. "I'll get the shoes later," she called through the door.

She dropped the towel and unzipped the bag, staring at the contents with no small amount of horror. There was… underwear inside of it. Underwear that Chase had purchased for her.

Which meant he had somehow managed to look at her breasts and evaluate their size. Not to mention her ass. And ass size.

She grabbed the pair of panties that were attached to a little hanger. Oh, they had no ass. So she supposed the size of hers didn't matter much.

She swallowed hard, taking hold of the soft material and rubbing her thumb over it. He would know exactly what she was wearing beneath the dress. Would know just how little that was.

He isn't going to think about it. Because he doesn't think about you that way.

He never had. He never would. And it was a damn good thing. Because where would they be if either of them acted on an attraction between them?

Up shit creek without a paddle or a friendship.

No, thank you. She was never going to touch him. She'd made that decision a long time ago. For a lot of reasons that were as valid today as they had been the very first time he'd ever made her stomach jump when she looked at him.

She was never going to encourage or act on the attraction that she occasionally felt for Chase. But she would take his expertise in sexual politics and use it to her advantage.

Oh, but those panties.

The bra wasn't really any less unsettling. Though at least it wasn't missing large swathes of fabric.

Still, it was very thin. And she had a feeling that a cool

ocean breeze would reveal the shape of her nipples to all and sundry.

Then again, maybe it was time all and sundry got a look at her nipples. Maybe if they had a better view, men would be a little more interested.

She scowled, wrenching the panties off the hanger and dragging them on as quickly as possible, followed closely by the bra. She was overthinking things. She was overthinking all of this. Had been from the moment Chase had walked into the barn. As evidenced by that lapse in the shower.

She had spent years honing her Chase Control. It was just this change in how they were interacting that was screwing with it. She was not letting this get inside her head, and she was not letting hot, unsettled feelings get inside her pants.

She pulled the garment bag away entirely, revealing a tight red dress slightly too reminiscent of what the woman he had been flirting with last night was wearing.

"Clearly you have a type, Chase McCormack," she muttered, beginning to remove the slinky scrap of material from the hanger.

She tugged it up over her hips, having to do a pretty intense wiggle to get it up all the way before zipping it into place. She took a deep breath, turned around. She faced her reflection in the mirror full-on and felt nothing but deflated.

She looked…well, her hair was wet and straggly, and she looked half-drowned. She didn't look curvy, or shimmery, or delightful.

This was the problem with tight clothes. They only made her more aware of her curve deficit.

Where the blonde last night had filled her dress out admirably, and in all the right places, on Anna this dress kind of looked like a piece of fabric stretched over an ironing board. Not really all that sexy.

She sighed heavily, trying to ignore the sinking feeling in her stomach.

Chase really was going to have to be a miracle worker in order to pull this off.

She didn't really want to show him. Instead, she found the idea of putting the coveralls back on a lot less reprehensible. At least with the coveralls there would still be some mystery. He wouldn't be confronted with just how big a task lay before him.

"Buck up," she said to herself.

So what was one more moment of feeling inadequate? Honestly, in the broad tapestry of her life it would barely register. She was never quite what was expected. She never quite fit. So why'd she expect that she was going to put on a sexy dress and suddenly be transformed into the kind of sex kitten she didn't even want to be?

She gritted her teeth, throwing open the bedroom door and walking out into the room. "I hope you're happy," she said, flinging her arms wide. "You get what you get."

She caught a movement out of the corner of her eye and turned her head, then recoiled in horror. It was even worse out here. Out here, there was a full-length mirror. Out here, she had the chance to see that while her breasts remained stunningly average, her hips and behind had gotten rather wide. Which was easy to ignore when you wore loose attire most days. "I look like the woman symbol on the door of a public restroom."

She looked over at Chase, who had been completely silent upon her entry into the room, and remained so. She glared at him. He wasn't saying anything. He was only staring. "Well?"

"It's nice," he said.

His voice sounded rough, and kind of thin.

"You're a liar."

"I'm not a liar. Put the shoes on."

"Do you even know what size I wear?"

"You're a size ten, which I know because you complain about how your big feet make it impossible for you to find anything in your size. And you're better off buying men's work boots. So yes, I know."

His words made her feel suddenly exposed. Well, his words in combination with the dress, she imagined. They knew each other a little bit too well. That was the problem. How could you impress a guy when you had spent a healthy amount of time bitching to him about your big feet?

"Fine. I will put on the shoes." He held them up, and her jaw dropped. "I thought you were taking me out to dinner."

"I am."

"Do I have to pay for it by working the pole at the Naughty Mermaid?"

"These are *nice* shoes."

"If you're a five-foot-two-inch Barbie like that chick you were talking to last night. I'm like…an Amazon in comparison."

"You're not an Amazon."

"I will be in those."

"Maybe that would bother some men. But you want a man who knows how to handle a woman. Any guy with half a brain is going to lose his mind checking out your legs. He's not going to care if you're a little taller than he is."

She tried her best to ignore the compliment about her legs. And tried even harder to keep from blushing.

"I care," she muttered, snatching the shoes from his hand and pondering whether or not there was any truth to her words as she did.

She didn't really date. So it was hard to say. But now that she was thinking about it, yeah. She was self-conscious about the fact that with pretty low heels she was eye level with half the men in town.

She finished putting the shoes on and straightened. It was like standing on a glittery pair of stilts. "Are you satisfied?" she asked.

"I guess you could say that." He was regarding her closely, his jaw tense, a muscle in his cheek ticking.

She noticed that he was still a couple of inches taller than her. Even with the shoes. "I guess you still meet the height requirement to be my dinner date."

"I didn't have any doubt."

"I don't know how to walk in these," she said.

"All right. Practice."

"Are you out of your mind? I have to *practice* walking?"

"You said yourself, you don't know how to walk in heels. So, go on. Walk the length of the room."

She felt completely awash in humiliation. She doubted there was another woman on the planet that Chase had ever had to instruct on walking.

"This is ridiculous."

"It's not," he said.

"All of women's fashion is ridiculous," she maintained. "Do you have to learn how to walk when you put on dress shoes? No, you do not. And yet, a full-scale lesson is required for me to go out if I want to wear something that's considered *feminine*."

"Yeah, it's sexist. And a real pain in the ass, I'm sure. It's also hot. Now walk."

She scowled at him, then took her first step, wobbling a bit. "I don't understand why women do this."

She took another step, then another, wobbling a little less each time. But the shoes did force her hips to sway, much more than they normally would. "Do you have any pointers?" she asked.

"I date women in heels, Anna. *I've* never walked in them."

"What happened to helping me be a woman?"

"You'll get the hang of it. It's like…I don't know, water-skiing maybe?"

"How is this like water-skiing?"

"You have to learn how to do it and there's a good likelihood you'll fall on your face?"

"Well, I take it all back," she said, deadpan. "These shoes aren't silly at all." She took another step, then another. "I feel like a newborn baby deer."

"You look a little like one, too."

She snorted. "You really need to up your game, Chase. If you use these lines on all the women you take out, you're bound to start striking out sooner or later."

"I haven't struck out yet."

"Well, you're still young and pretty. Just wait. Just wait until time starts to claim your muscular forearms and chiseled jawline."

"I figure by then maybe I'll have gotten the ranch back to its former glory. At that point women will sleep with me for my money."

She rolled her eyes. "It's nice to have goals."

In her opinion, Chase should have better goals for himself. But then, who was she to talk? Her current goal was to show her brothers that they were idiots and she could too get a date. Hardly a lofty ambition.

"Yes, it is. And right now my goal is for us not to miss our reservation."

"You made a…reservation?"

"I did."

"It's not like it's Valentine's Day or something. The restaurant isn't going to be full."

"Of course it won't be. But I figured if I made a reservation for the two of us, we could start a rumor, too."

"A rumor?"

"Yeah, because Ellie Matthews works at Beaches, and I believe she has been known to *service* your brother Mark."

Anna winced at the terminology. "True."

"I thought the news of our dining experience might make it back to him. Like I said, the more we can make this look organic, the better."

"No one ever need know that our relationship is in fact grown in a lab. And in no way GMO free," she said.

"Exactly."

"I don't have any makeup on." She frowned. "I don't have any makeup. At all."

"Right," he said. "I didn't really think of that."

She reached out and smacked him on the shoulder. "You're supposed to be my coach. You're failing me."

He laughed, dodging her next blow. "You don't need makeup."

She let out an exasperated sigh. "You're just saying that."

"In fairness, you did threaten to castrate me with your car keys earlier."

"I did."

"And you hit me just now," he pointed out.

"It didn't hurt, you baby."

He took a deep breath, and suddenly his expression turned sharp. "Believe me when I tell you you don't need makeup." He reached out, gripping her chin with his thumb and forefinger. His touch was like a branding iron, hot, altering. "As long as you believe it, everyone else will, too. You have to believe in yourself, Anna."

He released his hold on her, straightening. "Now," he said, his tone getting a little bit rougher, "let's go to dinner."

Chase felt like he had been tipped sideways and left walking on the walls from the moment that Anna had emerged from the bathroom at his house wearing that dress. Once she had put on those shoes, the feeling had only gotten worse.

But who knew that underneath those coveralls his best friend looked like that?

She had been eyeing herself critically, and his brain had barely been working at all. Because he didn't see anything to criticize. All he saw was the kind of figure that would make a man willingly submit to car key castration.

She was long and lean, toned from all the physical labor she did. Her breasts were small, but he imagined they would fit in a man's hand nicely. And her hips...well, using the same measurement used for her breasts, they would be about perfect for holding on to while a man...

Holy hell. He was losing his mind.

She was Anna. Anna Brown, his best friend in the entire world. The one woman he had never even considered going there with. He didn't want a relationship with the women he slept with. When your only criteria for being with a woman was orgasm, there were a lot of options available to you. For a little bit of satisfaction he could basically seek out any woman in the room.

Sex was easy. Connections were hard.

And so Anna had been placed firmly off-limits from day one. He'd had a vague awareness of her for most of his life. That was how growing up in a small town worked. You went to the same school from the beginning. But they had separate classes, plus at the time he'd been pretty convinced girls had cooties.

But that had changed their first year of high school. He'd ended up in metal shop with the prickly teen and had liked her right away. There weren't very many girls who cursed as much as the boys and had a more comprehensive understanding of the inner workings of engines than the teachers at the school. But Anna did.

She hadn't fit in with any of the girls, and so Chase and

Sam had been quick to bring her into their group. Over the years, people had rotated in and out, moved, gone their separate ways. But Chase and Anna had remained close.

In part because he had kept his dick out of the equation.

As they walked up the path toward Beaches, he considered putting his hand on her lower back. Really, he should. Except it was potentially problematic at the moment. Was he this shallow? Stick her in a tight-fitting dress and suddenly he couldn't control himself? It was a sobering realization, but not really all that surprising.

This was what happened when you spent a lot of time practicing no restraint when it came to sex.

He gritted his teeth, lifting his hand for a moment before placing it gently on her back. Because it was what he would do with any other date, so it was what he needed to do with Anna.

She went stiff beneath his touch. "Relax," he said, keeping his voice low. "This is supposed to look like a date, remember?"

"I should have worn a white tank top and a pair of jeans," she said.

"Why?"

"Because this looks… It looks like I'm trying too hard."

"No, it looks like you put on a nice outfit to please me."

She turned to face him, her brow furrowed. "Which is part of the problem. If I had to do this to please you, we both know that I would tell you to please yourself."

He laughed, the moment so classically Anna, so familiar, it was at odds with the other feelings that were buzzing through his blood. With how soft she felt beneath his touch. With just how much she was affecting him in this figure-hugging dress.

"I have no doubt you would."

They walked up the steps that led into the large white restaurant, and he opened the door, holding it for her. She looked at him like he'd just caught fire. He stared her down, and then she looked away from him, walking through the door.

He moved up next to her once they were inside. "You're going to have to seem a little more at ease with this change in our relationship."

"You're being weird."

"I'm not being weird. I'm treating you like a lady."

"What have you been treating me like for the past fifteen years?" she asked.

"A…bro."

She snorted, shaking her head and walking toward the front of the house where Ellie Matthews was standing, waiting for guests. "I believe we have a reservation," Anna said.

He let out a long-suffering sigh. "Yes," he confirmed. "Under my name."

Ellie's eyebrow shot upward. "Yes. You do."

"Under Chase McCormack and Anna Brown," Chase clarified.

"I know," she said.

Ellie needed to work on her people skills. "It was difficult for me to tell, since you look so surprised," Chase said.

"Well, I knew you were reserving the table for the two of you, but I didn't realize you were…reserving the table for *the two of you*." She was looking at Anna's dress, her expression meaningful.

"Well, I was," he said. "Did. So, is the table ready?"

She looked around the half-full dining area. "Yeah, I'm pretty sure we can seat you now."

Ellie walked them over to one of the tables by a side window that looked out over the Skokomish River where it fed into the ocean. The sun was dipping low over the water, the rays sparkling off the still surface of the slow-moving river. There were people milling along the wooden boardwalk that was bordered by docks on one side and storefronts on the other, before being split by the highway and starting again, leading down to the beach.

He looked away from the scenery, back at Anna. They had shared countless meals together, but this was different. Normally, they didn't sit across from each other at a tiny table complete with a freaking candle in the middle. Mood lighting.

"Your server will be with you shortly," Ellie said as she walked away, leaving them there with menus and each other.

"I want a burger," Anna said, not looking at the menu at all.

"You could get something fancier."

"I'll get it with a cheese I can't pronounce."

"I'm getting salmon."

"Am I paying?" she asked, an impish smile playing around the corners of her lips. "Because if so, you better be putting out at the end of this."

Her words were like a punch in the gut. And he did his best to ignore them. He swallowed hard. "No, *I'm* paying."

"I'll pay you back after. You're doing me a favor."

"The favor's mutual. I want to go to the fund-raiser. It's important to me."

"You still aren't buying my dinner."

"I'm not taking your money."

"Then I'm going to overpay for rent on the shop next month," she said, her tone uncompromising.

"Half of that goes to Sam."

"Then he gets half of it. But I'm not going to let you buy my dinner."

"You're being stubborn."

She leaned back in her chair, crossing her arms and treating him to that hard glare of hers. "Yep."

A few moments later the waiter came over, and Anna

ordered her hamburger, and the cheeses she wanted, by pointing at the menu.

"Which cheese did you get?" he asked, attempting to move on from their earlier standoff.

"I don't know." She shrugged. "I can't pronounce it."

They made about ten minutes of awkward conversation while they waited for their dinner to come. Which was weird, because conversation was never awkward with Anna. It was that dress. And those shoes. And his penis. That was part of the problem. Because, suddenly, it was actually interested in his best friend.

No, it is not. A moment of checking her out does not mean that you want to...do anything with her.

Exactly. It wasn't a big deal. It wasn't anything to get worked up about. Not at all.

When their dinner was placed in front of them, Anna attacked her sweet potato fries, probably using them as a displacement activity.

"Chase?"

Chase looked up and inwardly groaned when he saw Wendy Maxwell headed toward the table. They'd all gone to high school together. And he had, regrettably, slept with Wendy once or twice over the years after drinking too much at Ace's.

She was hot. But what she had in looks had been deducted from her personality. Which didn't matter when you were only having sex, but mattered later when you had to interact in public.

"Hi, Wendy," he said, taking a bite of his salmon.

Anna had gone very still across from him; she wasn't even eating her fries anymore.

"Are you... Are you on a date?" Wendy asked, tilting her head to the side, her expression incredulous.

Wendy wasn't very smart in addition to being not very nice. A really bad combination.

"Yes," he said, "I am."

"With Anna?"

"Yeah," Anna said, looking up. "The person sitting across from him. Like you do on a date."

"I'm just surprised."

He could see color mounting in Anna's cheeks, could see her losing her hold on her temper.

"Are you here by yourself?" Anna asked.

Wendy laughed, the sound like broken crystal being pushed beneath his skin. "No. Of course not. We're having a girls' night out." She eyed Chase. "Of course, that doesn't mean I'm going home with the girls."

Suddenly, Anna was standing, and he was a little bit afraid she was about to deck Wendy. Who deserved it. But he didn't really want to be at the center of a girl fight in the middle of Beaches.

That only worked in fantasies. Less so in real life.

But it wasn't Wendy whom Anna moved toward.

She took two steps, came to a stop in front of Chase and then leaned forward, grabbing hold of the back of his chair and resting her knee next to his thigh. Then she pressed her hand to his cheek and took a deep breath, making determined eye contact with him just before she let her lids flutter closed. Just before she closed the distance between them and kissed him.

Four

She was kissing Chase McCormack. Beyond that, she had no idea what the flying F-bomb she was doing. If there was another person in the room, she didn't see them. If there was a reason she'd started this, she didn't remember it.

There was nothing. Nothing more than the hot press of Chase's lips against hers. Nothing more than still, leashed power beneath her touch. She could feel his tension, could feel his strength frozen beneath her.

It was…intoxicating. Empowering.

So damn *hot*.

Like she was about to melt the soles of her shoes hot. About to come without his hands ever touching her body hot.

And that was unheard-of for her.

She'd kissed a couple of guys, and slept with one, and orgasm had never been in the cards. When it came to climaxes, she was her own hero. But damn if Chase wasn't about to be her hero in under thirty seconds, and with nothing more than a little dry lip-to-lip contact.

Except it didn't stay dry.

Suddenly, he reached up, curling his fingers around the back of her head, angling his own and kissing her hard, deep. With tongue.

She whimpered, the leg that was supporting her body melting, only the firm hold he had on her face, and the support of his chair, keeping her from sliding onto the ground.

The slick glide of his tongue against hers was the single sexiest thing she'd ever experienced in her life. And just like that, every little white lie she'd ever told herself about her attraction to Chase was completely and fully revealed.

It wasn't just a momentary response to an attractive man. Not something any red-blooded female would feel. Not just a passing anomaly.

It was real.

It was deep.

She was so screwed.

Way too screwed to care that they were making out in a fancy restaurant in front of people, and that for him it was just a show, but for her it was a whole cataclysmic, near-orgasmic shift happening in the region of her panties.

Seconds had passed, but they felt like minutes. Hours. Whole days' worth of life-changing moments, all crammed into something that probably hadn't actually lasted longer than the blink of an eye.

Then it was over. She was the one who pulled away and she wasn't quite sure how she managed. But she did.

She wasn't breathing right. Her entire body was shaking, and she was sure her face was red. But still, she turned and faced Wendy, or whichever mean girl it was. There were a ton of them in her nonhalcyon high school years and they all blended together. The who wasn't important. Only the what. The *what* being a kiss she'd just given to the hottest guy in town, right in front of someone who didn't think she was good enough. Pretty enough. Girlie enough.

"Yeah," she said, her voice a little less triumphant and a lot more unsteady than she would like, "we're here on a date. And he's going home with me. So I'd suggest you wiggle on over to a different table if you want to score tonight."

Wendy's face was scrunched into a sour expression. "That's okay, honey, if you want my leftovers, you're welcome to them."

Then she flipped her blond hair and walked back to her table, essentially acting out the cliché of every snotty girl in a teen movie.

Which was not so cute when you were thirty and not fifteen.

But, of course, since Wendy was gone, they'd lost the buffer against the aftermath of the kiss, and the terrible awkwardness that was just sitting there, seething, growing.

"Well, I think that started some rumors," Anna said, sitting back down and shoving a fry into her mouth.

"I bet," Chase said, clearing his throat and turning back toward his plate.

"My mouth has never touched your mouth directly before," she said, then stuffed another fry straight into her mouth, wishing it wasn't too late to stifle those ridiculous words.

He choked on his beer. "Um. No."

"What I mean is, we've shared drinks before. I've taken bites off your sandwiches. Literally sandwiches, not— I mean, whatever. The point is, we've germ-shared before. We just never did it mouth-to-mouth."

"That wasn't CPR, babe."

She made a face, hoping the disgust in her expression would disguise the twist low and deep in her stomach. "Don't call me babe just because I kissed you."

"We're dating, remember?"

"No one is listening to us talk at the table," she insisted.

"You don't know that."

Her heart was thundering hard like a trapped bird in her chest and she didn't know if she could look at him for another minute without either scurrying from the room like a frightened animal or grabbing him and kissing him again.

She didn't like it. She didn't like any of it.

It all felt too real, too raw and too scary. It all came from a place too deep inside her.

So she decided to do what came easiest. Exactly what she did best.

"I expected better," she told him, before taking a bite of her burger.

"What?"

"You're like a legendary stud," she said, after swallowing her food. "The man who every man wants to be and who every woman wants to be with. Blah, blah." She picked up another sweet potato fry.

"It wasn't good for you?" he asked.

"Six point five from the German judge. Who is me, in this scenario." She was a liar. She was a liar and she was a jerk, and she wanted to punch her own face. But the alternative was to show that she was breaking apart inside. That she had been on the verge of the kind of ecstasy she'd only ever imagined, and that she wanted to kiss him forever, not just for thirty seconds. And that was…damaging. It wasn't something she could admit.

"Six point five."

"Sorry." She lifted her shoulder and shoved the fry into her mouth.

They finished the rest of the dinner in awkward silence, which made her mad because things weren't supposed to be awkward between them. They were friends, dammit. She was starting to think this whole thing was a mistake.

She could bring Chase as her plus one to the charity thing without her brothers buying into it. She could lose the bet. The whole town could suspect she'd brought a friend because she was undatable and who even cared?

If playing this game was going to screw with their friendship, it wasn't worth it.

Chase paid the tab—she was going to pay the bastard back whether he wanted her to or not—and then the two of them walked outside. And that was when she realized her truck was back at his place and he was going to have to give her a ride.

That sucked donkey balls. She needed to get some Chase space. And it wasn't going to happen.

She wanted to go home and put on soft pajamas and watch *Seven Brides for Seven Brothers*. She needed a safe, flannel-lined space and the fuzzy comfort of an old movie. A chance to breathe and be vulnerable for a second where no one would see.

She was afraid Chase might have seen already.

They still didn't talk—all the way back out of town and to the McCormack family ranch, they didn't talk.

"My dirty clothes are in your house," she said at last, when they pulled into the driveway. "You can take me to the house first instead of the shop."

"I can wash them with mine," he said.

Her underwear was in there. That was not happening.

"No, I left them folded in the corner of the bathroom. I'd rather come get them. And put my shoes on before I try to drive home actually. How do people drive in these?" She tapped the precarious shoes against the floor of the pickup.

Chase let out a harsh-sounding breath. "Fine," he said. He sounded aggrieved, but he drove on past the shop to the house. He stopped the truck abruptly, throwing it into Park and killing the engine. "Come on in."

Now he was mad at her. Great. It wasn't like he needed

her to stroke his ego. He had countless women to do that. He had just one woman who listened to his bullshit and put up with all his nonsense, and in general stood by him no matter what. That was her. He could have endless praise for his bedroom skills from those other women. He only had friendship from *her*. So he could simmer down a little.

She got out of the truck, then wobbled when her foot hit a loose gravel patch. She clung tightly to the door, a very wussy-sounding squeak escaping her lips.

"You okay there, *babe*?" he asked, just to piss her off.

"Yeah, fine. Jerk," she retorted.

"What the hell, Anna?" he asked, his tone hard.

"Oh, come on, you're being weird. You can't pretend you aren't just because you're layering passivity over your aggression." She stalked past him as fast as her shoes would let her, walked up the porch and stood by the door, her arms crossed.

"It's not locked," he said, taking the stairs two at a time.

"Well, I wasn't going to go in without your permission. I have manners."

"Do you?" he asked.

"If I didn't, I probably would have punched you by now." She opened the door and stomped up the stairs, until her heel rolled inward slightly and she stumbled. Then she stopped stomping and started taking a little more consideration for her joints.

She was mad at him. She was mad at herself for being mad at him, because the situation was mostly her fault. And she was mad at him for being mad at her for being mad at him.

Mad, mad, *mad*.

She walked into the bathroom and picked up her stack of clothes, careful not to hold the greasy articles against her dress. The dress that was the cause of so many of tonight's problems.

It's not the dress. It's the fact that you kissed him and now you can't deal.

Rationality was starting to creep in and she was nothing if not completely irritated about that. It was forcing her to confront the fact that she was actually the one being a jerk, not him. That she was the one who was overreacting, and his behavior was all a response to the fact that she'd gone full Anna-pine, with quills out ready to defend herself at all costs.

She took a deep breath and sat down on the edge of his bed, trading the high heels for her sneakers, then collecting her things again and walking back down the stairs, her feet tingling and aching as they got used to resting flat once more.

Chase wasn't inside.

She opened the front door and walked out onto the porch.

He was standing there, the porch light shining on him like a beacon. His broad shoulders, trim waist…oh, Lord, his ass. Wrangler butt was a gift from God in her opinion and Chase's was perfect. Something she'd noticed before, but right now it was physically painful to look at him and not close the space between them. To not touch him.

This was bad. This was why she hadn't ever touched him before. Why it would have been best if she never had.

She had needs. Fuzzy-blanket needs. She needed to get home.

She cleared her throat. "I'm ready," she said. "I just… If you could give me a lift down to the shop, that would be nice. So that I'm not cougar food."

He turned slowly, a strange expression on his face. "Yeah, I wouldn't want you to get eaten by any mangy predators."

"I appreciate that."

He headed down the steps and got back into the truck,

and she followed, climbing into the cab beside him. He started the engine and maneuvered the truck onto the gravel road that ran through the property.

She rested her elbow on the armrest, staring outside at the inky black shadows of the pine trees, and the white glitter of stars in the velvet-blue sky. It was a clear night, unusual for their little coastal town.

If only her head was as clear as the sky.

It was full. Full of regret and woe. She didn't like that. As soon as Chase pulled up to the shop, she scrambled out, not waiting for him to put the vehicle in Park. She was heading toward her own vehicle when she heard Chase behind her.

"What are you doing?" she asked, turning to face him.

But her words were cut off by what he did next. He took one step toward her, closing the distance between them as he wrapped his arm around her waist and drew her up against his chest. Then, before she could protest, before she could say anything, he was kissing her again.

This was different than the kiss at the restaurant. This was different than…well, than any kiss in the whole history of the world.

His kiss tasted of the familiarity of Chase and the strangeness of his anger. Of heat and lust and rage all rolled into one.

She knew him better than she knew almost anyone. Knew the shape of his face, knew his scent, knew his voice. But his scent surrounding her like this, the feel of his face beneath her hands, the sound of that voice—transformed into a feral, passionate growl as he continued to ravish her—was an unknown. Was something else entirely.

Then, suddenly—just as suddenly as he had initiated it—the kiss was over. He released his hold on her, pushing her back. There was nothing but air between them now. Air and a whole lot of feelings. He was standing there, his hands planted on his lean hips, his chest rising and falling with each labored breath. "Six point five?" he asked, his tone challenging. "That sure as hell was no six point five, Anna Brown, and if you're honest with yourself, you have to admit that."

She sucked in a harsh, unsteady breath, trying to keep the shock from showing on her face. "I don't have to admit any such thing."

"You're a little liar."

"What does it matter?" she asked, scowling.

"How would you like it if I told you that you were only average compared to other women I've kissed?"

"I'd shut your head in the truck door."

"Exactly." He crossed his arms over his broad chest. "So don't think I'm going to let the same insults stand, honey."

"Don't *babe* me," she spat. "Don't *honey* me."

Triumph glittered in his dark eyes. The smugness so certain it was visible even in the moonlight. "Then don't kiss me again."

"You were the one who kissed me!" she shouted, throwing her arms wide.

"*This* time. But you started it. Don't do it again." He turned around, heading back toward his truck. All she could do was stand there and stare as he drove away.

Something had changed tonight. Something inside of her. She didn't think she liked it at all.

Five

"Now, I don't want to be insensitive or hurt your feelings, princess, but why are you being such an asshole today?"

Chase looked over at Sam, who was staring at him from his position by the forge. The fire was going hot and they were pounding out iron, doing some repairs on equipment. By hand. Just the way both of them liked to work.

"I'm not," Chase said.

"Right. Look, there's only room for one of us to be a grumpy cuss, and I pretty much have that position filled. So I would appreciate it if you can get your act together."

"Sorry, Sam, are you unable to take what you dish out every day?"

"What's going on with you and Anna?"

Chase bristled at the mention of the woman he'd kissed last night. Then he winced when he remembered the kiss. Well, *remembered* was the wrong word. He'd never forgotten it. But right now he was mentally replaying it, moment by moment. "What did you hear?"

Sam laughed. An honest-to-God laugh. "Do I look like I'm on the gossip chain? I haven't talked to anybody. It's just that I saw her leaving your house last night wearing a red dress and sneakers, and then saw her this morning when she went into the shop. She was pissier than you are."

"Anna is always pissy." Sam treated his statement to a prolonged stare. "It's not a big deal. It's just that her brothers bet her that she couldn't get a date. I figured I would help her out with that."

"How?"

"Well…" he said, hesitating about telling his brother the whole story. Sam wasn't looking to change the business on the ranch. He didn't care about their family legacy. Not like Chase did. But Chase had made promises to tombstones and he wasn't about to break them.

It was one of their main sources of contention. So he wasn't exactly looking forward to having this conversation with his older brother.

But it wasn't like he could hide it forever. He'd just sort of been hoping he could hide it until he'd shown up with investment money.

"That's an awfully long pause," Sam said. "I'm willing to bet that whatever you're about to say, I'm not going to like it."

"You know me well. Anna got invited to go to the big community charity event that the West family hosts every year. Now I want to make sure that we can extend our contract with them. Plus…doing horseshoes and gates isn't cutting it. We can move into doing details on custom homes. To doing art pieces and selling our work across the country, not just locally. To do that we need investors. And the West fund-raiser's a great place to find them. Plus, if I only have to wear a suit once and can speak to everyone in town that might be interested in a single shot? Well, I can't beat that."

"Dammit, Chase, you know I don't want to commit to something like that."

"Right. You want to continue on the way we always have. You want to shoe horses when we can, pound metal when the opportunity presents itself, build gates, or whatever else might need doing, then go off and work on sculptures and things in your spare time. But that's not going to be enough. Less and less is done by hand, and people aren't willing to pay for handcrafted materials. Machines can build cheaper stuff than we can.

"But the thing is, you can make it look special. You can turn it into something amazing. Like you did with my house. It's the details that make a house expensive. We can have the sort of clients who don't want work off an assembly line. The kind who will pay for one of a kind pieces. From art on down to the handles on their kitchen cabinets. We could get into some serious custom work. Vacation homes are starting to spring up around here, plus people are renovating to make rentals thanks to the tourism increase. But we need some investors if we're really going to get into this."

"You know I hate this. I don't like the idea of charging a ton of money for a...for a gate with an elk on it."

"You're an artist, Sam," he said, watching his brother wince as he said the words. "I know you hate that. But it's true."

"I hate that, too."

"You're talented."

"I hit metal with a hammer. Sometimes I shape it into something that looks nice. It's not really all that special."

"You do more than that and you know it. It's what people would be willing to pay for. If you would stop being such a nut job about it."

Sam rubbed the back of his neck, his expression shuttered. "You've gotten off topic," he said finally. "I asked you about Anna, not your schemes for exploiting my talents."

"Not really. The two are connected. I want to go to this

thing to talk to the Wests. I want to talk about investment opportunities and expanding contracts with other people deemed worthy of an invite. In case you haven't noticed, we weren't on that list."

"Yeah, I get that. But why would the lately not-so-great McCormacks be invited?"

"That's the problem. This place hasn't been what it was for a couple of generations, and when we lost Mom and Dad…well, we were teenagers trying to keep up a whole industry, and now we work *for* these people, not with them. I aim to change that."

"You didn't think about talking to me?" Sam asked.

"Oh, I did. And I decided I didn't want to have to deal with you."

Sam shot him an evil glare. "So you're going as Anna's date. And helping her win her bet."

"Exactly."

"And you took her out last night, and she went back to your place, and now she's mad at you."

Chase held his hands up. "I don't know what you're getting at—"

"Yes, you do." Sam crossed his arms. "Did you bang her?"

Chase recoiled, trying to look horrified at the thought. He didn't *feel* horrified at the thought. Which actually made him feel kind of horrified. "I did not."

"Is that why you're mad? Because you didn't?"

His brother was way too perceptive for a guy who pounded heavy things with other heavy things for a living.

"No," he said. "Anna is my friend. She's just a friend. We had a slight…altercation last night. But it's not that big a deal."

"Big enough that I'm worried with all your stomping around you're eventually going to fling the wrong thing and hit me with molten metal."

"Safety first," Chase said, "always."

"I bet you say that to your dates, too."

"You would, too, if you had any."

Sam flipped Chase the bird in response.

"Just forget about it," Chase said. "Forget about the stuff with the Wests, and let me deal with it. And forget about Anna."

When it came to that last directive, he was going to try to do the same.

Anna was dreading coming face-to-face with Chase again after last night. But she didn't really have a choice. They were still in this thing. Unless she called it off. But that would be tantamount to admitting that what had happened last night *bothered* her. And she didn't want to do that. More, she was almost incapable of doing it. She was pretty sure her pride would wither up and die if she did.

But Chase was coming by her shop again tonight, with some other kind of lesson in mind. Something he'd written down on that stupid legal pad of his. It was ridiculous. All of it was ridiculous.

Herself most of all.

She looked at the clock, gritting her teeth. Chase would be by any moment, and she was no closer to dealing with the feelings, needs and general restlessness that had hit her with the blunt force of a flying wrench than she had been last night.

Then, right on time, the door opened, and in walked Chase. He was still dirty from work today, his face smudged with ash and soot, his shirt sticking to his muscular frame, showing off all those fine muscles underneath. Yeah, that didn't help.

"How was work?" he asked.

"Fine. Just dealing with putting a new cylinder head on a John Deere. You?"

"Working on a gate."

"Sounds...fun," she said, though she didn't really think it sounded like fun at all.

She liked solving the puzzle when it came to working on engines. Liked that she had the ability to get in there and figure things out. To diagnose the situation.

Standing in front of a hot fire forging metal didn't really sound like her kind of thing.

Though she couldn't deny it did pretty fantastic things for Chase's physique.

"Well, you know it would be fine if Sam wasn't such a pain in the ass."

"Sure," she said, feeling slightly cautious. After last night, she felt like dealing with Chase was like approaching a dog who'd bitten you once. Only, in this case he had kissed her, not bitten her, and he wasn't a dog. That was the problem. He was just much too *much* for his own good. Much too much for her own good.

"So," she said, "what's on the lesson plan for tonight?"

"I sort of thought we should talk about...well, talking."

"What do you mean?"

"There are ways that women talk to men they want to date. I thought I might walk you through flirting."

"You're going to show me how to flirt?"

"Somebody has to."

"I can probably figure it out," she said.

"You think?" he asked, crossing his arms over his chest and rocking back on his heels.

His clear skepticism stoked the flames of her temper, which was lurking very close to the surface after last night. That was kind of her default. Don't know how to handle something? Don't know *what* you feel? Get angry at it.

"Come on. Men and women have engaged in horizontal naked kickboxing for millennia. I'm pretty sure flirting is a natural instinct."

"You're a poet, Anna," he said, his tone deadpan.

"No, I'm a tractor mechanic," she said.

"Yeah, and you talk like one, too. If you want to get an actual date, and not just a quick tumble in the back of a guy's truck, you might want to refine your art of conversation a little."

"Who says I'm opposed to a quick rough tumble in the back of some guy's truck?"

"You're not?" he asked, his eyebrows shooting upward.

"Well, in all honesty I would probably prefer my truck, since it's clean. I know where it's been. But why the hell not? I have needs."

He scowled. "Right. Well, keep that kind of talk to yourself."

"Does it make you uncomfortable to hear about my *needs*, Chase?" she asked, not quite sure why she was poking at him. Maybe because she felt so unsettled. She was kind of enjoying the fact that he seemed to be, as well. Really, it wouldn't be fair if after last night he felt nothing at all. If he had been able to one-up her and then walk away as though nothing had happened.

"It doesn't make me uncomfortable. It's just unnecessary information. Now, talking about your needs is probably something you shouldn't do with a guy, either."

"Unless I want him to fulfill those needs."

"You said you wanted to date. You want the kind of date who can go to these functions with you, right?"

"It's moot. You're going with me."

"This time. But be honest, don't you want to be able to go out with guys who belong in places like that?"

"I don't know," she said, feeling uncomfortable.

Truth be told, she wasn't all that comfortable thinking about her needs. Emotional, physical. Frankly, if it went beyond her need for a cheeseburger, she didn't really know how to deal with it. She hadn't dated in years. And she had been fine with that. But the truth of the matter was the only reason Mark and Daniel had managed to get to her when they had made this bet was that she was beginning to feel dissatisfied with her life.

She was starting a new business. She was assuming a new position in the community. She didn't just want to be Anna Brown, the girl from the wrong side of the tracks. She didn't just want to be the tomboy mechanic for the rest of her life. She wanted…more. It had been fine, avoiding relationships all this time, but she was thirty now. She didn't really want to be by herself. She didn't want to be alone forever.

Dear Lord, she was having an existential crisis.

"Fine," she said, "it might be nice to have somebody to date."

Marriage, family—she had no idea how she felt when it came to those things. But a casual relationship… That might be nice. Yes. That might be nice.

Last night, she had gone home and gotten under a blanket and watched an old movie. Sometimes, Chase watched old movies with her, but he did not get under the blankets with her. It would be nice to have a guy to be under the blanket with. Somebody to go home to. Or at least someone to call to come over when she couldn't sleep. Someone she could talk to, make out with. Have sex with.

"Fine," she said. "I will submit to your flirting lessons."

"All the girls submit to me eventually," he said, winking.

Something about that made her stomach twist into a knot. "Talking about too much information…"

"There," he said, "that was almost flirting."

She wrinkled her nose. "Was it?"

"Yes. We had a little bit of back and forth. There was some innuendo."

"I didn't make innuendo on purpose," she said.

"No. That's the best kind. The kind you sort of walk

into. It makes you feel a little dangerous. Like you might say the wrong thing. And if you go too far, they might walk away. But if you don't go far enough, they might not know that you want them."

She let out a long, frustrated growl. "Dating is complicated. I hate it. Is it too late for me to become a nun?"

"You would have to convert," he pointed out.

"That sounds like a lot of work, too."

"You can be pleasant, Anna. You're fun to talk to. So that's all you have to do."

"Natural to me is walking up to a hot guy and saying, 'Do you want to bone or what?'" As if she'd ever done that. As if she ever would. It was just…she didn't really know how to go about getting a guy to hook up with her any other way. She was a direct kind of girl. And nothing between men and women seemed direct.

"Fine. Let's try this," he said, grabbing a chair and pulling it up to her workbench before taking a seat.

She took hold of the back of the other folding chair in the space and moved it across from his, positioning herself so that she was across from him.

"What are you drinking?" he asked.

She laughed. "A mai tai." She had never had one of those. She didn't even know what it was.

"Excellent. I'm having whiskey, straight up."

"That sounds like you."

"You don't know what sounds like me. You don't know me."

Suddenly, she got the game. "Right. Stranger," she said, then winced internally, because that sounded a little bit more Mae West in her head, and just kind of silly when it was out of her mouth.

"You here with anyone?"

"I could be?" she said, placing her elbow on the workbench and tilting her head to the side.

"You should try to toss your hair a little bit. I dated this girl Elizabeth who used to do that. It was cute."

"How does touching my hair accomplish anything?" she asked, feeling irritated that he had brought another woman up. Which was silly, because the only reason he was qualified to give her these lessons was that he had dated a metric ton of women.

So getting mad about the thing that was helping her right now was a little ridiculous. But she was pretty sure they had passed ridiculous a couple of days ago.

"I don't know. It's cute. It looks like you're trying to draw my attention to it. Like you want me to notice."

"Which…lets you know that I want you in my pants?"

He frowned. "I guess. I never broke it down like that before. But that stands to reason."

She reached up, sighing as she flicked a strand of her hair as best she could. It was tied up in a loose bun and had fallen partway thanks to the intensity of the day's physical labor. Still, she had a feeling she did not look alluring. She had a feeling she looked like she'd been caught in a wind turbine and spit out the other end.

"Are you new in town?"

"I'm old in town," she said, mentally kicking herself again for being lame on the return volley.

"That works, too," Chase said, not skipping a beat. Yeah, there was a reason the man had never struck out before.

She started to chew on her lip, trying to think of what to say next.

"Don't chew a hole through it," he said, smiling and reaching across the space, brushing his thumb over the place her teeth had just grazed.

And everything in her stopped dead. His touch ignited her nerve endings, sending a brush fire down her veins and all through her body.

She hadn't been this ridiculous over Chase since she

was sixteen years old. Since then, she had mostly learned to manage it.

She pulled away slightly, her chair scraping against the floor. She laughed, a stilted, unnatural sound. "I won't," she said, her voice too loud.

"If you're going to chew on your lip," he said, "don't freak out when the guy calls attention to it or touches you. It looks like you're doing it on purpose, so you should expect a comment."

"Duh," she said, "I was. That was…normal."

She wanted to crawl under the chair.

"There was this girl Miranda that I—"

"Okay." She cut him off, growing more and more impatient with the comparisons. "I'm old in town, what about you?"

"I've been around."

"I bet you have been," she said.

"I'm not sure how I'm supposed to take that," he said, flashing her a lopsided grin.

"Right," she said, "because I don't know what I'm doing."

"Maybe this was a bad idea," he said. "I think you actually need to feel some chemistry with somebody if flirting's going to work."

His words were sharp, digging into her chest. *You actually had to feel some chemistry* to be able to flirt.

They had chemistry. She had felt it last night. So had he. This was his revenge for the six-point-five comment. At least, she hoped it was. The alternative was that he had really felt nothing when their lips attached. And that seemed…beyond unfair.

She had all this attraction for Chase that she had spent years tamping down, only to have it come roaring to the surface the moment she had begun to pretend there was more going on between them than just friendship. And then she had kissed him. And far from being a disappointment, he had superseded her every fantasy. The jackass. Then he had kissed her, kissed her because he was angry. Kissed her to get revenge. Kissed her in a way that had kept her awake all night long, aching, burning. And now he was saying he didn't have chemistry with her.

"It's just that usually when I'm with a girl it flows a little easier. The bar to the bedroom is a pretty natural extension. And all those little movements kind of lead into the other. The way they touch their hair, tilt their head, lean in for a kiss…"

Oh, that did it.

"The women that I usually hook up with tend to—"

"Right," she said, her tone hard. "I get it. They flip their hair and scrunch their noses and twitch at all the appropriate times. They're like small woodland creatures who only emerge from their burrows to satisfy your every sexual whim."

"Don't get upset. I'm trying to help you."

She snorted. "I know." Just then, she had no idea what devil possessed her. Only that one most assuredly did. And once it had taken hold, she had no desire to cast it back out again.

She was mad. Mad like Chase had been last night. And she was determined to get her own back.

"Elizabeth was good at flipping her hair. Miranda gave you saucy interplay like so." She stood up, taking a step toward him, meeting his dark gaze with her own. "But how did they do this?" She reached down, placing her hand between his thighs and rubbing her palm over the bulge in his jeans.

Oh, sweet Lord, there was more to Chase McCormack than met the eye.

And she had a whole handful of him.

Her brain was starting to scream. Not words so much as

a high-pitched, panicky whine. She had crossed the line. And there was no turning back.

But her brain wasn't running the show. Her body was on fire, her heart pounding so hard she was afraid it was going to rip a hole straight through the wall of her chest and flop out on the ground in front of him. Show him all its contents. Dammit, *she* didn't even want to see that.

But it was her anger that really pushed things forward. Her anger that truly propelled her on.

"And how," she asked, lowering herself slowly, scraping her fingernails across the line of his zipper, before dropping to her knees in front of him, "did they do this?"

Six

For one blinding second, Chase thought that he was engaged in some sort of high-definition hallucination.

Because there was no way that Anna had just put her hand...there. There was no way that she was kneeling down in front of him, looking at him like she was a sultry-eyed seductress rather than his best friend, still dirty from the workday, clad in motor-oil-smudged coveralls.

He blinked. Then he shook his head. She was still there. And so was he.

But he was so hard he could probably pound iron with his dick right about now.

He knew what he should do. And just now he had enough sense left in his skull to do it. But he didn't want to. He knew he should. He knew that at the end of this road there was nothing good. Nothing good at all. But he shut all that down. He didn't think of the road ahead.

He just let his brain go blank. He just sat back and watched as she trailed her fingers up the line of his zipper, grabbing hold of his belt buckle and undoing it, her movements clumsy, speaking of an inexperience he didn't want to examine too closely.

He didn't want to examine any of this too closely, but he was powerless to do anything else.

Because everything around the moment went fuzzy as the present sharpened. Almost painfully.

His eyes were drawn to her fingers as she pulled his zipper down, to the short, no-nonsense fingernails, the specks of dirt embedded in her skin. That should…well, he had the vague idea it should turn him off. It didn't. Though he had a feeling that getting a bucket of water thrown on him while he sat in the middle of an iceberg naked wouldn't turn him off at this point. He was too far gone.

He was holding his breath. Every muscle in his body frozen. He couldn't believe that she would do what it appeared she might be doing. She would stop. She had to stop. He needed her to stop. He needed her to never stop. To keep going.

She pressed her palm flat against his ab muscles before pushing her hand down inside his jeans, reaching beneath his underwear and curling her fingers around him. His breath hissed through his teeth, a shudder racking his frame.

She looked up at him, green eyes glittering in the dim shop light. She had a smudge of dirt on her face that somehow only highlighted her sharp cheekbones, somehow emphasized her beauty in a way he hadn't truly noticed it before. Yes, last night in the red dress she had been beautiful, there was no doubt about that. But for some reason, her femininity was highlighted wrapped in these traditionally masculine things. By the backdrop of the mechanic shop, the evidence of a day's hard work on her soft skin.

She tilted her chin up, her expression one of absolute challenge. She was waiting for him to call it off. Waiting for him to push her away. But he wasn't going to. He reached out, forking his fingers through her hair and tightening them, grabbing ahold of the loose bun that sat high on her head. Her eyes widened, her lips going slack. He didn't pull her away. He didn't draw her closer. He just held on tight, keeping his gaze firmly focused on hers. Then he released her. And he waited.

She licked her lips slowly, an action that would have been almost comically obvious coming from nearly anyone else. Not Anna.

Then she squeezed him gently before drawing her hand back. He should be relieved. He was not.

But her next move was not one he anticipated. She grabbed hold of the waistband of his jeans and underwear, pulling them down slowly, exposing him. She let out a shaky, shuddering breath before leaning in and flicking her tongue over the head of his arousal.

"Hell." He wasn't sure at first if he had spoken it out loud, not until he heard it echoing around him. It was like cursing in a church somehow, wrong considering the beauty of the gift he was about to receive.

Still, he couldn't think of anything else as she drew the tip of her tongue all the way down to the base of his shaft before retracing her path. She shifted, and that was when he noticed her hands were shaking. Fair enough, since he was shaking, too.

She parted her lips, taking him into her mouth completely, her lips sliding over him, the wet, slick friction almost too much for him to handle. He didn't know what was wrong with him. If it was the shock of the moment, if it was just that he was this base. Or if there was some kind of sick, perverted part of him that took extra pleasure in the fact that this was wrong. That he should not be letting his best friend touch him like this.

Because he'd had more skilled blow jobs. There was no

question about that. This didn't feel good because Anna was an expert in the art of fellatio. Far from it.

Still, his head was about to blow off. And he was about to lose all of his control. So there was something.

Maybe it was just her.

She tilted her head to the side as she took him in deep, giving him a good view of just what she was doing. And just who was doing it. He was so aware of the fact that it was Anna, and that most definitely added a kick of the forbidden. Because he knew this was bad. Knew it was wrong.

And not many things were off-limits to him. Not many things had an illicit quality to them. He had kind of allowed himself to take anything and everything that had ever seemed vaguely sexy to him.

Except for her.

He shoved that thought in the background. He didn't like to think of Anna that way, and in general he didn't.

Sure, in high school, there had been moments. But he was a guy. And he had spent a lot of time with Anna. Alone in her room, alone in his. He had a feeling that half the people who had known them had imagined they were getting it on behind the scenes. Friends with benefits, et cetera. In reality, the only benefit to their friendship had been the fact that they'd been there for each other. They had never been there for each other in this way.

Maybe that's what was wrong with him.

Of course, nothing felt wrong with him right now. Right now, pleasure was crackling close to the surface of his skin and it was shorting out his brain. All he could do was sit back and ride the high. Embrace the sensations that were boiling through his blood. The magic of her lips and tongue combined with a shocking scrape of her teeth against his delicate skin made him buck his hips against her even as he tried to rein himself in.

But he was reaching the end of his control, the end of himself. He reached down, cupping her cheek as she continued to pleasure him, as she continued to drive him wild, urging him closer to the edge of control he hadn't realized he possessed.

He felt like he lived life with the shackles off, but she was pushing him so much further than he'd been before that he knew he'd been lying to himself all this time.

He'd been in chains, and hadn't even realized it.

Maybe because of her. Maybe to keep himself from touching her.

She gripped him, squeezing as she tasted him, pushing him straight over the edge. He held on to her hair, harder than he should, as a wave of pleasure rode up inside of him. And when it crashed he didn't ride it into shore. Oh, hell no. When it crashed it drove him straight down to the bottom of the sea, the impact leaving him spinning, gasping for breath, battered on the rocks.

But dammit all, it was worth it. Right now, it was worth it.

He knew that any moment the feeling would fade and he would be faced with the stark horror of what he'd just done, of what he'd just allowed to happen. But for now, he was foggy, floating in the kind of mist that always blanketed the ocean on cold mornings in Copper Ridge.

And he would cling to it as long as possible.

Oh, dear God. What had she done? This had gone so far beyond the kiss to prove they had chemistry. It had gone so far past the challenge that Chase had thrown down last night. It had gone straight into Crazy Town, next stop You Messed Up the Only Friendship You Hadville.

In combination with the swirling panic that was wrapping its claws around her and pulling her into a spiral was the fuzzy-headed lingering arousal. Her lips felt swollen, her body tingling, adrenaline still making her shake.

She regretted everything. She also regretted nothing.

The contradictions inside her were so extreme she felt like she was going to be pulled in two.

One thing her mind and body were united on was the desire to go hide underneath a blanket. This was definitely the kind of situation that necessitated hiding.

The problem was, she was still on her knees in front of Chase. Maybe she could hide under his chair.

What are you doing? Why are you falling apart? This isn't a big deal. He has probably literally had a thousand blow jobs.

This one didn't have to be that big a deal. Sure, it was the first one she had ever given. But he didn't have to know that, either.

If she didn't treat it like a big deal, it wouldn't be a big deal. They could forget anything had ever happened. They could forget that in a moment of total insanity she had allowed her anger to push her over the edge, had allowed her inability to back down from a challenge to bring them to this place. And that was all it was—the fact that she was absolutely unable to deal with that blow to her pride. It was nothing else. It couldn't be anything else.

She rocked back on her heels, planting her hands flat on the dusty ground before rising to her feet. She felt dizzy. She would go ahead and blame that on the speed at which she had stood up.

"I think it's safe to say we have a little bit more chemistry than you thought," she said, clearing her throat and brushing at the dirt on her pants.

He didn't say anything. He just kept sitting there, looking rocked. And he was still exposed. She did her very best to look at the wall behind him. "I can still see your..."

He scrambled into action, standing and tugging his

pants into place, doing up his belt as quickly as possible. "I think we're done for the day."

She nodded. "Yeah. Well, *you* are."

She could feel the distance widening between them. It was what she needed, what she wanted, ultimately. But for some reason, even as she forced the breach, she regretted it.

"I don't… What just happened?"

She laughed, crossing her arms and cocking her hip out to the side. "If you have to ask, maybe I didn't do a very good job." The bolder she got, the more she retreated inside. She could feel herself tearing in two, the soft vulnerable part of her scrambling to get behind the brash, bold outward version that would spare her from any embarrassment or pain.

"You're…okay?"

"Why wouldn't I be okay?"

"Because you just…"

She laughed. Hysterically. "Sure. But let's not be ridiculous about it. It isn't like you punched me in the face."

Chase looked stricken. "Of course not. I would never do that."

"I know. I'm just saying, don't act like you punched me in the face when all I did was—"

"There's no need to get descriptive. I was here. I remember."

She snorted. "You should remember." She turned away from him, clenching her hands into fists, hoping he didn't notice that they were shaking. "And I hope you remember it next time you go talking about us not having chemistry."

"Do you *want* us to have chemistry?"

She whirled around. "No. But I have some pride. You were comparing me to all these other women. Well, compare that."

"I…can't."

She planted her hands on her hips. "Damn straight."

"We can't… We can't do this again," he said, shaking his head and walking away.

For some reason, that made her feel awful. For some reason, it hurt. Stabbed like a rusty knife deep in her gut.

"I don't want to do it again. I mean, you're welcome, but I didn't exactly get anything out of it."

He stopped, turning to face her, his expression tense. "I didn't ask you to do anything."

"I'm aware." She shook her head. "I think we're done for tonight."

"Yeah. I already said that."

"Well," she said, feeling furious now, "now I'm saying it."

She was mad at herself. For taking it this far. For being upset, and raw, and wounded over something that she had chosen to do. Over his reaction, which was nothing more than the completely predictable response. He didn't want her. Not really.

And she knew that. This evening's events weren't going to change it. An orgasm on the floor of the shop she rented from him was hardly going to alter the course of fifteen years of friendship.

An orgasm. Oh, dear Lord, what had she done? She really had to get out of here. There was no amount of bravado left in her that would save her from the meltdown that was pending.

"I have to go."

She was gone before he had a chance to protest. He should be glad she was gone. If she had stayed, there was no telling what he might have done. What other stupid bit of nonsense he might have committed.

He had limited brainpower at the moment. All of his blood was still somewhere south of his belt.

He turned, surveying the empty shop. Then, in a fit of rage, he kicked something metal that was just to the right of the chair. And hurt his foot. And probably broke the thing. He had no idea if it was important or not. He hoped it wasn't. Or maybe he hoped it was. She deserved to have some of her tractor shit get broken. What had she been thinking?

He hadn't been able to think. But it was a well-known fact that if a man's dick was in a woman's mouth, he was not doing much problem solving. Which meant Chase was completely absolved of any wrongdoing here.

Completely.

He gritted his teeth, closing his eyes and taking in a sharp breath. He was going to have to figure out how to get a handle on himself between now and the next time he saw Anna. Because there was no way things could continue on like this. There weren't a whole lot of people who stuck around in his world. There had never been a special woman. After the death of his and Sam's parents, relatives had passed through, but none of them had put down roots. And, well, their parents, they might not have chosen to leave, but they were gone all the same. He couldn't afford to lose anyone else. Sam and Anna were basically all he had.

Which meant when it came to Sam's moods and general crankiness, Chase just dealt with it. And when it came to Anna…no more touching. No more… No more of any of that.

For one second, he allowed himself to replay the moment when she had unzipped his pants. When she had leaned forward and tasted him. When that white-hot streak of release had undone him completely.

He blinked. Yeah, he knew what he had been thinking. That it felt good. Amazing. Too good to stop her. But physical pleasure was cheap. A friendship like theirs represented years of investment. One simply wasn't worth sacrificing the other for. And now that he was thinking clearly he realized that. So that meant no more. No more. Never.

Next time he saw her, he was going to make sure she knew that,

Seven

Anna was beneath three blankets, and she was starting to swelter. If she hadn't been too lazy to sit up and grab hold of her ice-cream container, she might not be quite so sweaty.

The fact that she was something of a cliché of what it meant to be a woman behind closed doors was not lost on her. Blankets, old movies, Ben & Jerry's. But hey, she spent most of the day up to her elbows in engine grease, so she supposed she was entitled to a few stereotypes.

She reached her spoon out from beneath the blankets and scraped the top of the ice cream in the container, gathering up a modest amount.

"Oklahoma!" she sang, humming the rest of the line while taking the bite of marshmallow and chocolate ice cream and sighing as the sugar did its good work. Full-fat dairy products were the way to happiness. Or at least the best way she knew to stop from obsessing.

Her phone buzzed and she looked down, cringing when

she saw Chase's name. She swiped open the lock screen and read the message.

In your driveway. Didn't want to give you a heart attack.

Why are you in my dr—

She didn't get a chance to finish the message before there was a knock on her front door.

She closed her eyes, groaning. She really didn't want to deal with him right now. In fact, he was the last person on earth she wanted to deal with. He was the reason she was currently baking beneath a stack of blankets, seeking solace in the bosom of old movies.

Still, she couldn't ignore him. That would make things weirder. He was still her best friend, even if she had— Well, she wasn't going to think about what she had. If she ignored him, it would only cater to the weirdness. It would make events from earlier today seem more important than they needed to be. They did not need to be treated as though they were important.

Sure, she had never exactly done *that* with a man. Sure, she hadn't even had sexual contact of any kind with a man for the past several years. And sure, she had never had that kind of contact with Chase. But that was no reason to go assigning meaning. People got ribbons and stickers for their first trips to the dentist. They did not get them for giving their first blow job.

She groaned. Then she rolled off the couch, pushing herself into a standing position before she padded through the small living area to the entryway. She jerked the door open, pushing her hair out of her face and trying to look casual.

Too late, she realized that she was wearing her pajamas. Which were perfectly decent, in that they covered every inch of her body. But they were also baggy, fuzzy and covered in porcupines.

All things considered, it just wasn't the most glorious of moments.

"Hello," she said, keeping her body firmly planted in the center of the doorway.

"Hi," he returned. Then he proceeded to study her pajamas.

"Porcupines," she informed him, just for something to say.

"Good choice. Not an obvious one."

"I guess not. Considering they aren't all that cuddly. But neither am I. So maybe it's a more obvious choice than it originally appears."

"Maybe. We'll have to debate animal-patterned pajama philosophy another time."

"I guess. What exactly did you come here to debate if not that?"

He stuffed his hands in his pockets. "Nothing. I just came to…check on you."

"Sound of body and mind."

"I see that. Except you're in your pajamas at seven o'clock."

"I'm preparing for an evening in," she said, planting her hand on her hip. "So pajamas are logical."

"Okay."

She frowned. "I'm fine."

"Can I come in?"

She was frozen for a moment, not quite sure what to say. If she let him come in…well, she didn't feel entirely comfortable with the idea of letting him in. But if she didn't let him in, then she would be admitting that she was uncomfortable letting him in. Which would betray the fact that she actually wasn't really all that okay. She didn't want to do that, either.

No wonder she had avoided sexual contact for so long. It introduced all manner of things that she really didn't want to deal with.

"Sure," she said finally, stepping to the side and allowing him entry.

He just stood there, filling up the entry. She had never really noticed that before. How large he was in the small space of her home. Because he was Chase, and his presence here shouldn't really be remarkable. It was now.

Because things had changed. She had changed them. She had kissed him the other day, and then…well, she had changed things.

"There. You are in," she said, moving away from him and heading back into the living room. She took a seat on the couch, picking up the remote control and muting the TV.

"Movie night?"

"Every night is movie night with enough popcorn and a can-do attitude."

"I admire your dedication. What's on?"

"Oklahoma!"

He raised his brows. "You haven't seen that enough times?"

"There is no such thing as seeing a musical too many times, Chase. Multiple viewings only enhance the experience."

"Do they?"

"Sing-alongs, of course."

"I should have known."

She smiled, putting a blanket back over her lap, thinking of it as a sort of flannel shield. "You should know these things about me. Really, you should know everything about me."

He cleared his throat, and the sudden awkwardness made her think of all the things he didn't know about her.

And the things that he did know. It hit her then—of course, right then, as he was standing in front of her—just how revealing what had happened earlier was.

Giving a guy pleasure like that…well, a woman didn't do that unless she wanted him. It said a lot about how she felt. About how she had felt for an awfully long time. No matter that she had tried to quash it, the fact remained that she did feel attraction for him. Which he was obviously now completely aware of.

Silence fell like a boulder between them. Crushing, deadly.

"Anyway," she said, the transition as subtle as a landslide. "Why exactly are you here?"

"I told you."

"Right. Checking on me. I'm just not really sure why."

"You know why," he said, his tone muted.

"You check on every woman you have…encounters with?"

"You know I don't. But you're not every woman I have encounters with."

"Still. I'm an adult woman. I'm neither shocked nor injured."

She was probably both. Yes, she was definitely perilously close to being both.

He shifted, clearly uncomfortable. Which she hated, because they weren't uncomfortable with each other. Ever. Or they hadn't been before. "It would be rude of me not to make sure we aren't…okay."

She patted herself down. "Yes. Okay. Okay?"

"No," he said.

"No? What the hell, man? I said I'm fine. Do we have to stand around talking about it?"

"I think we might. Because I don't think you're fine."

"That's bullshit, McCormack," she said, rising from the couch and clutching her blanket to her chest. "Straight-up bullshit. Like you stepped in a big-ass pile somewhere out there and now you went and dragged it into my house."

"If you were fine, you wouldn't be acting like this."

"I'm sorry, how did you want me to act?"

"Like an adult, maybe?" he said, his dark brows locking together.

"Um, I am acting like an adult, Chase. I'm pretending that a really embarrassing mistake didn't happen, while I crush my regret and uncertainty beneath the weight of my caloric intake for the evening. What part of that isn't acting like an adult?"

"We're friends. This wasn't some random, forgettable hookup."

"It is so forgettable," she said, her voice taking on that brash, loud quality that hurt her own ears. That she was starting to despise. "I've already forgotten it."

"How?"

"It's a penis, Chase, not the Sistine Chapel. My life was hardly going to be changed by the sight of it."

He reached forward, grabbing hold of her arm and drawing her toward him. "Stop," he bit out, his words hard, his expression focused.

"What are you doing?" she asked, some of her bravado slipping.

"Calling you on *your* bullshit, Anna." He lowered his voice, his tone no less deadly. She'd never seen Chase like this. He didn't get like this. Chase was fun, and light. Well, except for last night when he'd kissed her. But even then, he hadn't been quite this serious. "I've known you for fifteen years. I know when your smile is hiding tears, little girl. I know when you're a whole mess of feelings behind that brick wall you put up to keep yourself separate from the world. And I sure as hell know when you aren't fine. So don't stand there and tell me that it didn't change anything, that it didn't mean anything. Even if you gave out BJs every day with lunch—and I know you don't—that would have still mattered because it's *us*. And we don't do that. It changed something, Anna, and don't you dare pretend it didn't."

No. *No.* Her brain was screaming again, but this time she knew for sure what it was saying. It was all denial. She didn't want him to look at her as if he was searching for something, didn't want him to touch her as if it was only the beginning of something more. Didn't want him to see her. To see how scared she was. To see how unnerved and affected she was. To see how very, very not brave she was beneath the shield she held up to keep the world out.

He already knows it's a shield. And you're already screwed ten ways, because you can't hide from him and you never could.

He'd let her believe she could. And now he'd changed his mind. For some reason it was all over now. Well, she knew why. It had started with a dress and high heels and ended with an orgasm in her shop. He was right. It had changed things.

And she had a terrible, horrible feeling more was going to change before they could go back to normal.

If they ever could.

"Well," she said, hearing her voice falter. Pretending she didn't. "I don't think anything needs to change."

"Enough," he said, his tone fierce.

Then, before she knew what was happening, he'd claimed her lips again in a kiss that ground every other kiss that had come before it into dust, before letting them blow away on the wind.

This was angry. Intense. Hot and hard. And it was happening in her house, in spite of the fact that she was holding a blanket and *Oklahoma!* was on mute in the background. It was her safe space, with her safe friend, and it was being wholly, utterly invaded.

By him.

It was confronting and uncomfortable and scary as hell. So she responded the only way she could. She got mad, too.

She grabbed hold of the front of his shirt, clinging to him tightly as she kissed him back. As she forced her tongue between his lips, claiming him before he could stake his claim on her.

She shifted, scraping her teeth lightly over his bottom lip before biting down. Hard.

He growled, wrapping his arms around her waist. She never felt small. Ever. She was a tall girl with a broad frame, but she was engulfed by Chase right now. His scent, his strength. He was all hard muscle against her, his heart thundering beneath her hands, which were pinned between their bodies.

She didn't know what was happening, except that right now, kissing him might be safer than trying to talk to him.

It certainly felt better.

It let her be angry. Let her push back without saying anything. And more than that…he was an amazing kisser. He had taken her from zero to almost-there with one touch of his lips against hers.

He slid his hand down her back, cupping her butt and bringing her up even harder against him so she could feel him. All of him. And just how aroused he was.

He wanted her. Chase wanted her. Yes, he was pissed. Yes, he was…trying to prove a point with his tongue or whatever. But he couldn't fake a hard-on like that.

She was angry, but it was fading. Being blotted out by the arousal that was crackling in her veins like fireworks.

Suddenly, she found herself being lifted off the ground, before she was set down on the couch, Chase coming down over her, his expression hard, his eyes sharp as he looked down at her.

He pressed his hand over her stomach, pushing the hem of her shirt upward.

She should stop him. She didn't.

She watched as his strong, masculine hand pushed her shirt out of the way, revealing a wedge of skin. The contrast alone was enough to drive her crazy. Man, woman. Innocuous porcupine pajamas and sex.

Above all else, above anything else, there was Chase. Everything he made her feel. All of the things she had spent years trying *not* to feel. Years running from.

She couldn't run. Not now. Not only did she lack the strength, she lacked the desire. Because more than safety, more than sanity, she wanted him. Wanted him naked, over her, under her, *in* her.

He gripped the hem of her top and wrenched it over her head, the movement sudden, swift. As though he had reached the end of his patience and had no reserve to draw upon. That left her in nothing more than those ridiculous baggy pajama pants, resting low on her hips. She didn't have anything sexier underneath them, either.

But Chase didn't look at all disappointed. He didn't look away, either. Didn't have a faraway expression on his face. She wasn't sure why, but she had half expected to look up at him and be able to clearly identify that he was somewhere else in his mind, with someone else. But he was looking at her with a sharp focus, a kind of single-mindedness that no man, no *one*, had ever looked at her with before.

He knew. He knew who she was. And he was still hot for her. Still hard for her.

"You are so hot," he said, pressing his hand flat to her stomach and drawing it down slowly, his fingertips teasing the sensitive skin beneath the waistband. "And you don't even know it, do you?"

Part of her wanted to protest, wanted to fight back, because that was what she did. Instead, everything inside of her just kind of went limp. Melted into a puddle. "N-no."

"You should know," he said, his voice low, husky. A shot of whiskey that skated along her nerves, warming her, sending a kick of heat and adrenaline firing through her blood. "You should know how damn sexy you are. You're the kind of woman who could make a man lose his mind."

"I could?"

He laughed, but it wasn't full of humor. It sounded tortured. "I'm exhibit A."

He shifted his hips forward, his hard length pressing up against that very aroused part of her that wanted more of him. Needed more of him. She gasped. "Soon," he said, the promise in his words settling a heavy weight in her stomach. Anticipation, terror. Need.

He continued to tease her, his fingertips resting just above the line of her panties, before he began to trail his hand back upward. He rested his palm over her chest, reaching up and tracing her lower lip with his thumb.

She darted her tongue out, sliding the tip of it over his skin, tasting salt, tasting Chase. A flavor that was becoming familiar.

Then she angled her head, taking his thumb into her mouth and sucking hard. His hips arched forward hard, his cock making firm contact, sending a shower of sparks through her body as he did.

"You're going to be the death of me," he said, every word raw, frayed.

"I might say the same about you," she said, her voice thick, unrecognizable. She didn't know who she was right now. This creature who was a complete and total slave to sexual sensation. Who was so lost in it, she could feel nothing else. No sense of self-preservation, no fear kicking into gear and letting her know that she needed to put her walls up. That she needed to go on the defense.

She was reduced. She had none of that. And she didn't even care.

"You're a miracle," he said, tracing the line of her collarbone with the tip of his tongue. "A damn *miracle*, do you know that?"

"What?"

"The other day I told you you didn't look like a miracle. I was a fool. And I was wrong. Every inch of you is a miracle, Anna Brown."

Those words were like being submerged in warm water, feeling it flow over every inch of her, a kind of deep, soul-satisfying comfort that she really, really didn't want. Or rather, she didn't *want* to want it. But she did, bad enough that she couldn't resist.

But it was all a little too heavy. All a little too much. Still, she didn't have the strength to turn him away.

"Kiss me."

She said that instead of *get the hell out of my house*, and instead of *we can't do this*, because it was all she had strength for. Because she needed that kiss. And maybe, just maybe, if they didn't talk, she could make it through.

Chase—gentleman that he was—obliged her.

He angled his head, reaching up to cup her breast as he did, his mouth crashing down on hers just as his palm skimmed her nipple. She gasped, arching up against him, the combination of sensations almost too much to handle.

Yeah, she did not remember sex being like this. Granted, it had been a million years, but she would have remembered if it had come anywhere close to this. And her conclusion most certainly wouldn't have been that it was vaguely boring and a little bit gross. Not if it had even been in the same ballpark as what she was feeling now.

There was no point in comparing. There was just flat out no comparison.

He kissed her, long, deep and hard; he kissed her until she couldn't breathe. Until she thought she was going to die for wanting more. He kissed her until she was dizzy. And when he abandoned her mouth, she nearly wept. Until he lowered his head and skimmed his tongue over one hardened bud, until he drew it between his lips and sucked hard, before scraping her sensitized flesh with his teeth.

She arched against him, desperate for more. Desperate for satisfaction. Satisfaction he seemed intent on withholding.

"I'm so close," she said, panting. "Just do it now." Then it would be over. Then she would have what she needed, and the howling, yawning ache inside of her would be satisfied.

"No," he said, his tone authoritative.

"What do you mean no?"

"Not yet. You're not allowed to come yet, Anna. I'm not done."

His words, the calm, quiet command, made everything inside of her go still. She wanted to fight him. Wanted to rail against that cruel denial of her needs, but she couldn't.

Not when this part of him was so compelling. Not when she wanted so badly to see where complying would lead.

"We're not done," he said, tracing her nipple with the tip of his tongue, "until I say we are." He lifted his head so that their eyes met, the prolonged contact touching something deep inside of her. Something that surpassed the physical.

He kissed her again, and as he did, he pulled his T-shirt over his head, exposing his incredible body to her.

Her mouth dried, and other parts of her got wet. Very, very wet.

"Oh, sweet Lord," she said, pressing her hand to his chest and drawing her fingertips down over his muscles, his chest hair tickling her skin as she did.

It was a surreal moment. So strange and fascinating. To touch her best friend like this. To see his body this way, to know that—right now—it wasn't off-limits to her. To know that she could lean forward and kiss that beautiful, perfect dip just next to his hip bone. Suddenly, she was seized with the desire to do just that. And she didn't have to fight it.

She pushed against him, bringing herself into a sitting position, lowering her head and pressing her lips to his heated skin.

"Oh, no, you don't," he said, his voice rough. He took hold of her wrist, drawing her up so that she was on her knees, eye to eye with him on the couch. "We're not finishing it like that," he said.

"Damn straight we aren't," she said. "But that doesn't mean I didn't want to get a little taste."

"You give way too much credit to my self-control, honey."

"You give too much credit to mine. I've never…" She stared at his chest instead of finishing her sentence. "It's like walking into a candy store and being told I can have whatever I want. Restraint is not on the menu."

"Good," he said, leaning in, kissing her, nipping her lower lip. "Restraint isn't what I want."

He wrapped his arm around her, drawing her up against him, her bare breasts pressing against his hard chest, the hair there abrading her nipples in the most fantastic, delicious way.

And then he was kissing her again, slow and deep as his hand trailed down beneath the waistband of her pants, cupping her ass, squeezing her tight. He pushed her pants down over her hips, taking her panties with them, leaving her completely naked in front of him.

He stood up, taking his time looking at her as he put his hands on his belt buckle.

Nerves, excitement, spread through her. She didn't know where to look. At the harsh, hungry look on his face, at the beautiful lines of muscle on his perfectly sculpted torso. At the clear and aggressive arousal visible through his jeans.

So she looked at all of him. Every last bit. And she didn't have time to feel embarrassed that she was sitting there naked as the day she was born, totally exposed to him for the first time.

She was too fascinated by him in this moment. Too fascinated to do anything but stare at him.

This was Chase McCormack. The man that women lost their minds—and their dignity—over on a regular basis. This was Chase McCormack, the sex god who could—and often did—have any woman he pleased.

She had known Chase McCormack, loyal friend and confidant, for a very long time. But she realized that up until now, she had never met *this* Chase McCormack. It was a strange, dizzying realization. Exhilarating.

And she was suddenly seized by the feeling that right now, he was hers. All hers. Because who else knew both sides of him? Did anyone?

She was about to.

"Get your pants off, McCormack," she said, impatience overriding common sense.

"You don't get to make demands here, Anna," he said.

"I just did."

"You want to try giving orders? You have to show me you can follow them." His eyes darkened, and her heart hammered harder, faster. "Spread your legs," he said, his words hard and uncompromising.

She swallowed. There was that embarrassment that she had just been so proud she had bypassed. But this was suddenly way outside her realm of experience. It was one thing to sit there in front of him naked. It was quite another to deliberately expose herself the way he was asking her to. She didn't move. She sat there, frozen.

"Spread your legs for me," he repeated, his voice heavy with that soft, commanding tone. "Or I put my clothes on and leave."

"You wouldn't," she said.

"You don't know what I'm capable of."

That was true. In this scenario, she really didn't know him. He was a stranger, except he wasn't.

Actually, if he had been a stranger, all of this would've been a lot easier. She could have spread her legs and she wouldn't have worried about how she looked. Wouldn't have worried about the consequences. If a stranger saw her do something like that, was somehow unsatisfied and then walked away, well, what did it matter? But this was Chase. And it mattered. It mattered so very much.

His hands paused on his belt buckle. "I'm warning you, Anna. You better do as you're told."

For some reason, that did not make her want to punch him. For some reason, she found herself sitting back on the couch, obeying his command, opening herself to him, as adrenaline skittered through her system.

"Good girl," he said, continuing his movements, pushing his jeans and underwear down his legs and exposing his entire body to her for the first time. And then, it didn't matter so much that she was sitting there with her thighs open for him. Because now she had all of him to look at.

The light in his eyes was intense, hungry, and he kept them trained on her as he reached down and squeezed himself hard. His jaw was tense, the only real sign of just how frayed his control was.

"Beautiful," he said, stroking himself slowly, leisurely, as he continued to gaze at her.

"Are you just going to look? Or are you going to touch?" She wasn't entirely comfortable with this. With him just staring. With this aching silence between them, and this deep, overwhelming connection that she felt.

There were no barriers left. There was no way to hide. She was vulnerable, in every way. And normally she hated it. She kind of hated it now. But that vulnerability was wrapped in arousal, in a sharp, desperate need unlike anything she had ever known. And so it was impossible to try to put distance between them, impossible to try to run away.

"I'm going to do a lot more than look," he said, dropping down to his knees, "and I'm going to do a hell of a lot more than touch." He reached out, sliding his hands around to her ass, drawing her forward, bringing her up toward his mouth.

"Chase," she said, the short, shocked protest about the only thing she managed before the slick heat of his tongue assaulted that sensitive bundle of nerves at the apex of her thighs. "You don't have to…"

He lifted his head, his dark eyes meeting her. "Oh, I know I don't have to. But you got to taste me, and I think turnabout is fair play."

"But that wasn't…"

"What?"

"It's just that men…"

"Expect a lot more than they give. At least some of them. Anyway, as much as I liked what you did for me—and don't get me wrong, I liked it a lot—you have no idea how much pleasure this gives me."

"How?"

He leaned in, resting his cheek on her thigh. "The smell of you." He leaned closer, drawing his tongue through her slick folds. "The taste of you," he said. "You."

And then she couldn't talk anymore. He buried his face between her legs, his tongue and fingers working black magic on her body, pushing her harder, higher, faster than she had imagined possible. Yeah, making out with Chase had been enough to nearly give her an orgasm. This was pushing her somewhere else entirely.

In her world, orgasm had always been a solo project. Surrendering the power to someone else, having her own pleasure not only in someone else's hands but in his complete and utter control, was something she had never even thought possible for her. But Chase was proving her wrong.

He slipped a finger deep inside of her as he continued to torture her with his wicked mouth, then a second, working them in and out of her slick channel while he teased her with the tip of his tongue.

A ball of tension grew in her stomach, expanded until she couldn't breathe. "It's too much," she gasped.

"Obviously it's not enough yet," he said, pushing her harder, higher.

And when the wave broke over her, she thought she was done for. Thought it was going to drag her straight out to sea and leave her to die. She couldn't catch her breath as pleasure assaulted her, going on and on, pounding through her like a merciless tide, battering her against the rocks, leaving her bruised, breathless.

And when it was over, Chase was looming over her, a condom in his hand.

She felt like a creature without its shell. Sensitive, completely unprotected. She wanted to hide from him, hide from this. But she couldn't. How could she? The simple truth was, they still weren't done. They had gone only part of the way. And if they didn't finish this, she would always wonder. He would, too.

She imagined that—whether or not he admitted it—was why he had come here tonight in the first place.

They had opened the lid on Pandora's box. And they couldn't close it until they had examined every last dirty, filthy sin inside of it.

Even though she thought it might kill her, she knew that they couldn't stop now.

He tore open the condom, positioning the protection over the blunt head of his arousal, rolling it down slowly.

She was transfixed. The sight of his own hand on his shaft so erotic she could hardly stand it.

She would pay good money to watch him shower, to watch his hands slide over all those gorgeous muscles. To watch him take himself in hand and lead himself to completion.

Oh, yeah. That was now her number-one fantasy. Which was a problem, because it was a fantasy that would never be fulfilled.

Don't think about that now. Don't think about it ever.

He leaned in, kissing her, guiding her so that she was lying down on the couch, then he positioned himself between her legs, testing the entrance to her body before thrusting forward and filling her completely.

She closed her eyes tight, unable to handle the feeling of being invaded by him, both in body and in her soul.

"Look at me," he said.

And once more, she was completely helpless to do anything other than obey.

She opened her eyes, her gaze meeting his, touching her down deep, where his hands never could.

And then he kissed her, soft, gentle. That kind of tenderness that had been missing from her life for so long. The kind that she had always been too embarrassed to ask for from anyone. Too embarrassed to show that she needed. That she desperately craved.

But Chase knew. Because he was Chase. He just knew.

He flexed his hips again, his pelvis butting up against her, sending a shower of sparks through her body. There was no way she was ready to come again. Except he kept moving, creating new sensations inside of her, deeper than what had come before.

It shouldn't be possible for her to have another orgasm now. Not after the first one had stripped her so completely. But apparently tonight, nothing was impossible.

There was something different about this. About the two of them, working toward pleasure together. This wasn't just her giving it out to him, or him reciprocating. This was something they were sharing.

She focused on pieces of him. The intensity in his eyes. The way the tendons in his neck stood out, evidence of the control he was exerting. She looked at his hand, up by her head, grabbing hold of one of the blankets she had been using, clinging tightly to it, as though it were his lifeline.

She looked down at his throat, at the pulse beating there.

All these close, intimate snapshots of this man that she knew better than anyone else.

Her chest felt heavy, swollen, and then it began to expand. She was convinced that she was going to break apart. All of these feelings, all of this pleasure. It was just too much. She couldn't handle it.

"Please," she begged. "Please."

He released his grip on the blanket to grasp her hips, holding her steady as he pounded harder into her, as he pounded them both toward release. Toward salvation. It was too much. It needed to end. It was all she could think. She was begging him inside. *End it, Chase. Please, end it.*

Orgasm latched on to her throat like a wild beast, gripping her hard, violently, shaking her, pleasure exploding over her. Ugly. Completely and totally beyond control.

And then Chase let out a hoarse cry, freezing above her as he thrust inside her one last time, shivering, shaking as his own release took hold.

They were captive to it together. Powerless to do anything but wait until the savage beast was finished having its way. Until it was ready to move on.

And when it was over, only the two of them were left.

Just the two of them. Chase and Anna. No clothes, no shields.

She remembered the real reason she hadn't had sex since that first time. It had nothing to do with how good or bad it had felt. Nothing to do with what a jerk she'd been after.

It had been this. This feeling of being unable to hide. But with the other guy, it had been easy to regroup. Easy to pretend she felt nothing.

She couldn't do that with Chase. She was defenseless.

And for the first time in longer than she could remember, a tear slid down her cheek.

Eight

He couldn't swear creatively enough. He had just screwed his best friend's brains out on a couch in her living room. On top of what might be the world's friendliest, most nonsexual-looking blanket. With a Rodgers and Hammerstein musical on the TV in the background.

And then she had started crying. She had started crying, and she had wiggled out from beneath him and gone into the bathroom. Leaving him alone.

He had been sitting there by himself for a full thirty seconds attempting to reconcile all of these things.

And then he sprang into action.

He got up—still bare-ass naked—and walked down the hall. "Anna!" He didn't hear anything. And so he pounded on the bathroom door. "Anna!"

"I'm in the bathroom, dumbass!" came the terse, watery reply.

"I know. That's why I'm knocking on the bathroom door."

"Go away."

"No. I'm not going to go away. You need to talk to me."

"I don't want to talk."

"Anna, dammit, did I hurt you?"

He got nothing in return but silence. Then he heard the lock rattle, and the door opened a crack. One green eye looked up at him, accusing. "No."

"Why are you hiding?" He studied the eye more closely. It was red-rimmed. Definitely still weeping a little bit.

"I don't know," she said.

"Well…you had me convinced that I… Anna, it happened really fast."

"Not *that* fast. Believe me, I've had faster."

"You wanted all of that…? I mean…"

She laughed. Actually laughed, pushing the door open a little bit wider. "After my emphatic… After all the *yes-ing*… You can honestly ask whether or not I wanted it?"

"I have a lot of sex," he said. "I don't see any point in beating around the bush there. And women have had a lot of reactions to the sex. But I can honestly say none of them have ever run away crying. So, yeah, I'm feeling a little bit shaky right now."

"You're shaky? I'm the one that's crying."

"And if I was alone in this…if I pushed you further than you wanted to go…I'm going to have to ask Sam to fire up the forge and prepare you a red-hot poker so you can have your way with me in an entirely different manner."

"I wanted it, Chase." Her tone was muted.

"Then why are you crying?"

"I'm not very experienced," she said.

"Well, I mean, I know you don't really hook up."

"I've had sex once. One other time."

He was stunned. Stunned enough that he was pretty sure Anna could have put her index finger on his chest, given a light push and knocked him flat on his ass. "Once."

"Sure. You remember Corbin. And that whole fiasco.

Where I kind of made fun of his…lack of…attributes and staying power in the hall at school. And…basically ensured that no guy would ever touch me ever again."

"Right." He remembered that.

"Well, I didn't really get what the fuss was about."

"But you… I mean, you've had…"

"Orgasms? Yes. Almost every day of my life. Because I am industrious, and red-blooded, and self-sufficient."

He cleared his throat, trying to ignore the shot of heat that image sent straight through his blood. Anna. Touching herself.

What the hell was happening to him? Well, there was nothing happening. It had damn well *happened*. On the couch in Anna's living room.

He could never look at her again without seeing her there, obeying his orders. Spreading her thighs for him so that he could get a good look at her. Yeah, he could never unsee that. Wasn't sure if he wanted to. But where the hell did he go from here? Where did they go?

There were a lot of women he could have sex with, worry-free. Anna wasn't one of them. She was a rare, precious thing in his life. Someone who knew him. Who knew all about how affected he and Sam had been by the loss of their parents.

Someone he never had to explain it to because she'd been there.

He didn't like explaining all that. So the solution was keep the friends that were there when it happened, and make sure everyone else was temporary.

Which meant Anna couldn't be temporary. She was part of him. Part of his life. A load-bearing wall on the structure that was Chase McCormack. Remove her, and he would crumble.

That was why she had always stayed a friend. Why he had never done anything like this with her before. It wasn't because of her coveralls, or her don't-step-on-the-grass demeanor. Or even because she'd neatly neutered the reputation of the guy she'd slept with in high school.

It was because he needed her friendship, not her body.

But the problem was now he knew what she looked like naked.

He couldn't get that image out of his head. And he didn't even want to.

Same with the image of all her self-administered, industrious climaxes.

Damn his dirty mind.

"Okay," he said, taking a step away from the door. "Why don't you come out?"

"I'm naked."

"So am I."

She looked down. "So you are."

"We need to talk."

"Isn't it women who are supposed to require conversation after basic things like sex?"

"I don't know. Because I never stick around long enough to find out. But this is different. This is you and me, Anna, and I will be damned if I let things get messed up over a couple of orgasms."

She chewed her lower lip. She looked…well, she looked young. And she didn't look too tough. It made him ache. "They were pretty good ones."

"Are you all right?"

"I'm fine. It's just that all of this is a little bit weird. And I'm not really experienced enough to pretend that it isn't."

"Right." The whole thing about her having been with only one guy kind of freaked him out. Made him feel like he was responsible for some things. Big things, like what she would think of sex from this day forward. And then there was the bone-deep possessiveness. That he was the first one in all this time… He should hate it. It should scare him. It should not make him feel…triumph.

He was triumphant, dammit. "Why haven't you slept with anyone else?"

She lifted a shoulder. "I told you. I didn't really think my first experience was that great."

"So you just never…"

"I'm also emotionally dysfunctional, in case you hadn't noticed."

A shocked laugh escaped his lips. "Right. Same goes."

"I don't know. Sex kind of weirds me out. It's a lot of closeness."

"It doesn't have to be," he pointed out. It felt like a weird thing to say, though, because what they'd done just now had been the epitome of closeness.

"It just all feels…raw. And…it was good. But I think that's kind of why it bothered me."

"I don't want it to bother you."

"Well, the other thing is it was *you*. You and me, like you said. We don't do things like this. We hang out, we drink beer. We don't screw."

"Turns out we're pretty compatible when it comes to the screwing." He wasn't entirely sure this was the time to make light of what had just happened. But he was at sea here. So he had to figure out some way to talk to her. He figured he would make his best effort to treat her like he always did.

"Yeah," she said, finally pushing her way out of the bathroom. "But I'm not really sure there's much we can do with that."

He felt like he was losing his grip on something, something essential, important. Like he was on a rope precariously strung across the canyon, trying to hang on and not fall to his doom. Not fall to *their* doom, since she was right there with him.

What she was saying should feel like safety. It didn't. It felt like the bottom of the damn canyon.

"I don't know if that's the way to handle it."

"You don't?" she asked, blinking.

Apparently. He hadn't thought that statement through before it had come out of his mouth. "Yeah. Look, you kissed me yesterday. You gave me…oral pleasure earlier. And now we've had sex. Obviously, this isn't going away. Obviously, there's some attraction between us that we've never really acknowledged before."

"Or," she said, "someone cast a spell on us. Yeah, we drank some kind of sex potion. Makes you horny for twenty-four hours and then goes away."

"Sex potion?"

"It's either that or years of repressed lust, Chase. Pick whichever one makes you most comfortable."

"I would go with sex potion if I thought such a thing existed." He took a deep breath. "You know there's a lot of people that think men and women can't just be friends. And I've always thought that was stupid. Maybe this is why. Maybe it's because eventually, something happens. Eventually, the connection can't just be platonic. Not when you've spent so long in each other's company. Not when you're both reasonably attractive and single."

She snorted. "*Reasonably* attractive. What happened to me being a *damn miracle*?"

"I was referring to myself when I said reasonably. I'd hate to sound egotistical."

"Honestly, Chase, after thirty years of accomplished egotism, why worry about it now?"

He looked down at her. She was stark naked, standing in front of him, and he felt like he was in front of the pastry display case at Pie in the Sky. He wanted to sample everything, and he didn't know where to start.

But he couldn't do anything about that now. He was

trying to make amends. Dropping to his knees in front of her and burying his face between her legs probably wouldn't help with that.

He could feel his dick starting to wake up again. And since he was naked he might as well just go ahead and shout his intentions at her, because he wouldn't be able to hide them.

He couldn't look at her and not get hard, though. A new development in their relationship. But then, so was standing in front of each other without clothes.

"You're beautiful," he said, unable to help himself.

She wasn't as curvy as the women he usually gravitated toward. Her curves were restrained, her waist slim, with no dramatic sweep inward, just a slow build down to those wide, gorgeous hips that he now had fantasies about grabbing hold of while he pumped into her from behind. Her breasts were small but perfection in his mind. More would just be more.

He couldn't really imagine how he had ever looked at her face and found it plain. He had to kick his own ass mentally for that. He had been blind. Someone with unrefined, cheap taste. Who thought that if you stuck rhinestones and glitter on something, that meant it was prettier. But that wasn't Anna. She was simple, refined beauty. Something that only a connoisseur might appreciate. She was like a sunset over the ocean in comparison to a gaudy ballroom chandelier. Both had their strong points. But one was real, deep. Priceless instead of expensive.

That was Anna.

Something about those thoughts made a tightening sensation start in his gut and work its way up to his chest.

"Maybe what happened was just inevitable," he said, looking at her again.

"I can't really disprove that," she said, shifting uncomfortably. "You know, since it happened. I really need to put my clothes on."

"Do you have to?"

She frowned. "Yes. And you do, too. Because if we don't…"

"We'll have sex again."

The words stood between them, stark and far too true for either of their liking.

"Probably not," she said, sounding wholly unconvinced.

"Definitely yes."

She sighed heavily. "Chase, you can have sex with any-one you want. I'm definitely hard up. If you keep walking around flashing that thing, I'm probably going to hop on for a ride, I'll just be honest with you. But I understand if I'm not half as irresistible to you as you are to me."

Anger roared through him, suddenly, swiftly. And just like earlier, when she'd thrown her walls up and tried to drive a wedge between them, he found himself moving to-ward her. Moving to break through. He growled, backing her up against the wall, almost sighing in relief when his hardening cock met up with her soft skin, when her small breasts pressed against his chest. He grabbed hold of her hands, drawing them together and lifting them up over her head. "Let's get one thing straight, Anna," he said. "You are irresistible to me. If you weren't irresistible to me, I would still be at home. I never would have come here. I never would have kissed you. I never would have touched you. Don't you dare put yourself down. If this is because of your brothers, because of your dad…"

She closed her eyes, looking away from him. "Don't. It's not that."

"Then what is it? Why don't you think you can have this?"

"There's nothing to have. It's just sex. You mean the world to me. And just because I'm…suddenly unable to handle my hormones, I'm not going to compromise our friendship."

"It doesn't have to compromise it," he said, lowering his voice.

"What are you suggesting? We can't have a relationship with each other. We don't have those kinds of feelings for each other. A relationship is more than sex. It's romance and all kinds of stuff that I'm not even sure I want."

"I don't want it, either," he said. "But we're going to see each other. Pretty much every day. Not just because of the stupid bet. Not just because of the charity event. I'd call all that off right now if I thought it was going to ruin our friendship. But the horse has left the stable, Anna, well and truly. It's not going back in." He rolled his hips forward, and she gasped. "See what I mean? And if you were resistible? Then sure, I would tell you that we could just be done. We could pretend it didn't happen. But you're not. So I can't."

She opened her eyes again, looking up at him. "Then what are we doing?"

"You've heard of friends with benefits. Why can't we do that? I mean, I would never have set out to have that relationship. Because I don't think it's very smart. But… it's a little bit late for smart."

"Friends with benefits. As in…we stay friends by day and we screw each other senseless by night?"

Gah. That about sent him over the edge. "Yeah."

"Until what? Until…"

"Until you get that other date. Until the charity thing. As long as we're both single, why not? You're working toward the relationship stuff. You said you didn't want to be alone anymore. So, maybe this is good in the meantime. I know you're both industrious and red-blooded, and can get those orgasms all by yourself." He rolled his hips again and, much to his satisfaction, a small moan of pleasure escaped her lips. "But are they this good?"

"No," she said, her tone hushed.

"This is possibly the worst idea in the history of the world. But hell, you wanted to get some more experience… I'm offering to give it to you." The moment he said the words he wanted to bite his tongue off. The idea of giving Anna more experience just so she could go and do things with other men? That made him see red. Made him feel violent. Jealous. Things he never felt.

But what other option was there? He couldn't keep her. Not like this. But he couldn't let her go now.

He was messed up. *This* was messed up.

"I guess… I guess that makes sense. You know, until earlier today I'd never even given a guy a blow job."

"You're killing me," he said, closing his eyes.

"Well, I don't want you to die. You just offered me your penis for carnal usage. I want you alive."

"So that's it? My penis has now become the star of the show. Wow, how quickly our friendship has eroded."

"Our friendship is still solid. I think it just goes to prove how solid your dick is."

"With romantic praise like that, how are you still single?"

"I have no idea. I spout sonnets effortlessly."

He leaned forward, kissing her, a strange, warm sensation washing over him. He was kissing Anna. And it didn't feel quite as rushed and desperate as all the other times before it. A decision had been made. This wasn't a hasty race against sanity. This wasn't trying to get as much satisfaction as possible squeezed into a moment before reality kicked in. This was…well, in the new world order, it was sanctioned.

Instantly, he was rock hard again, ready to go, even though it'd been only a few minutes since his last orgasm. But there was one problem. "I don't have a condom," he said, cursing and pushing himself away from her. "I don't suppose the woman who has been celibate for the past thirteen years has one?"

"No," she said, sagging against the wall. "You only carry one on you?"

"Yeah. I'm not superhuman. I don't usually expect to get it on more than once in a couple of hours."

"But you were going to with me?"

He looked down at his very erect cock. "Does this answer your question?"

"Yeah."

"Well, then." He let out a heavy sigh.

"You could stay and watch...*Oklahoma!* with me."

He nodded slowly. He should stay and watch *Oklahoma!* with her. If he didn't, it kind of made a mockery of the whole friends-with-benefits thing. Because, before the sex, he would have stayed with her to watch a movie, of course. To hang out, because she was one of his favorite people on earth to spend time with. Even if her taste in movies was deeply suspect.

Of course, he didn't particularly want to stay now, because she presented the temptation that he could not give in to.

"Unless you have to work early tomorrow."

"I really do," he said.

"Thank God."

His eyebrows shot up. "You want to get rid of me?"

"I don't really want to hang out with you when I know I can't have you."

"I felt the same way, but I didn't want to say it. I thought it seemed kind of offensive."

Strangely, she smiled. "I'm not offended. I'm not offended at all. I kind of like being irresistible."

Instead of leaving, he knew that he could drive down to the store and buy a box of condoms. And he seriously considered it. The problem with that was there had to be some boundaries. Some limits. He was pretty sure being so horny and desperate that you needed to buy condoms right away instead of just waiting until you had protection on hand probably didn't fit within the boundaries of friends with benefits.

"I'll see you tomorrow, then."

She nodded. "See you tomorrow."

Nine

By the time Anna swung by the grocery store in the afternoon, she was feeling very mature, and very proud of herself. She was having a no-strings sexual relationship with her friend. And she was going to buy milk, cheese and condoms. Because she was mature and adult and completely fine with the whole situation. Also, mature.

She grabbed a cart and began to slowly walk up and down the aisles. She was not making sure that no one she knew was around. Because, of course, she wasn't at all embarrassed to be in the store looking for milk, cheese and—incidentally—prophylactics. She was *thirty*. She was entitled to a little bit of sexual release. Anyway, no one was actually watching her.

She swallowed hard, trying to remember exactly which aisle the condoms were in. She had never bought any. Ever. In her entire life.

She had been extremely tempted to make a dash to the store last night when Chase had discovered he didn't have any more protection, but she had imagined that was just a little bit too desperate. She was going to be nondesperate about this. Very chill. And not like a woman who was a near virgin. Or like someone who was so desperate to jump her best friend's bones it might seem like there were deeper emotions at play. There were not.

The strong feelings she had were just…in her pants. Pants feelings. That's it.

Last night's breakdown had been purely because she was unaccustomed to sex. Just a little post-orgasmic release. That's all it was. The whole thing was a release. Post-orgasmic tears weren't really all that strange.

She felt bolstered by that thought.

She turned down the aisle labeled Family Planning and made her way toward the condoms. Lubricated. Extra-thin. Ribbed. There were options. She had to stand there and seriously ponder ribbed. She should have asked Chase what he had used last night. Because whatever that had been had been perfect.

"Anna." The masculine voice coming from her left startled her.

She turned and—to her utter horror—saw her brother Mark standing there.

"Hi," she said, taking two steps away from the condom shelf, as though that would make it less obvious why she was in the aisle. Whatever. They were adults. Neither of them were virgins and they were both aware of that.

Still, she needed some distance between herself and anything that said "ribbed for her pleasure" when she was standing there talking to her brother.

"Haven't seen you in a couple days."

"Well, you pissed me off last time I saw you."

He lifted a shoulder. "Sorry."

He probably was, too.

"Hey, whatever. I win your bet."

His brows shot up. "I heard a rumor about you and Chase McCormack kissing at Beaches, but I was pretty sure that…" His eyes drifted toward the condoms. *"Really?"*

Dying of embarrassment was a serious risk at the moment, but she was caught. Completely and totally caught. And as long as she was drowning in a sea of horror…well, she might as well ride the tide.

If he needed proof her date with Chase was real, she imagined proof of sex was about the best there was.

She took a fortifying breath. "Really," she said, crossing her arms beneath her breasts. "It's happening. I have a date. I have more than a date. I have a whole future full of dates because I have a relationship. With Chase. You lose."

"I'm supposed to believe that you and McCormack are suddenly—" his eyes drifted back to the condoms again *"—that."*

"You don't have to believe it. It's true. He's also going to be my date to the charity gala that I'm invited to. I will take my payment in small or large bills. Thank you."

"I'm not convinced."

"You're not convinced?" She moved closer to the shelf and grabbed a box of condoms. "I am caught in the act."

"Convenient," he said, grabbing his own box.

She made a face. "It's not convenient. It happened."

"You're in love with him?"

The question felt like a punch to the stomach. She did not like it. She didn't like it at all. More than that, she had no idea what to say. *No* seemed…wrong. *Yes* seemed worse. And she wasn't really sure either answer was true.

You can't love Chase.

She couldn't not love him, either. He was her friend, after all. Of course she wasn't in love with him.

Her stomach twisted tight. No. She did not love him. She didn't do love. At all. Especially not with him. Because he would never…

"You look like you just got slapped with a fish," Mark said, and, to his credit, he looked somewhat concerned.

"I… Of course I love him," she said. That was a safe answer. It was also true. She did love him. As a friend. And… she loved his body. And everything about him as a human being. Except for the fact that he was a man slut who would never settle down with any woman, much less her.

Why not you?

No. She was not thinking about this. She wasn't thinking about any of this.

"Tell you what. If you're still together at the gala, you get your money."

"That isn't fair. That isn't what we agreed on."

He lifted a shoulder. "I know. But I also didn't expect you to grab your best friend and have him be your date. That still seems suspicious to me, regardless of…purchases."

"You didn't put any specifications on the bet, Mark. You can't change the rules now."

"We didn't put any specifications on it saying I couldn't."

"Why do you care?"

He snorted. "Why do you care?"

"I have pride, jackass."

"And I don't trust Chase McCormack. If you're still together at the gala, you get your money. And if he hurts you in any way, I will break his neck. After I pull his balls off and feed them to the sharks."

It wasn't very often that Mark's protective side was on display. Usually, he was too busy tormenting her. Their childhood had been rough. Their father didn't have any idea how to show affection to them, and as a result none of them were very good at it, either. Still, she never doubted that—even when he was a jerk—Mark cared about her.

"That's not necessary. Chase is my best friend. And now…he's more. He isn't going to hurt me."

"Sounds to me like he has the potential to hurt you worse than just about anybody."

His words settled heavily in the pit of her stomach. She should be able to brush them off. Because she and Chase were in a relationship. She and Chase were friends with benefits. And nothing about that would hurt at all.

"I'll be fine."

"If you need anything, just let me know."

"I will."

He lifted the condom box. "We'll pretend this didn't happen." Then he turned and started to walk away.

"Pretend what didn't happen?" She pulled her own box of condoms up against her chest and held it tightly. "See? I've already forgotten. Mostly because I can't afford therapy. At least not until you pay me the big bucks at the gala."

"We'll see," he said, walking out of sight.

She turned, chucking the box into her cart and making her way quickly down to the milk aisle. Chase wasn't going to hurt her, because Mark was wrong. They were only friends, and she quashed the traitorous flame in her stomach that tried to grow, tried to convince her otherwise.

She wasn't going to get hurt. She was just going to have a few orgasms and then move on.

That was her story, and she was sticking to it.

"I'm taking you dancing tonight," Chase said as soon as Anna picked up the phone.

"Did you bump your head on an anvil today?"

He supposed he shouldn't be that surprised to hear Anna's sarcasm. After last night—vulnerability, tears—he'd had a feeling that she wasn't going to be overly friendly today. In fact, he'd guessed that she would have transformed into one of the little porcupines that were on her pajamas. He had been right.

"No," he said. "I'm just following the lesson plan. I said I was taking you out, and so I am."

"You know," she said, her voice getting husky, "I'm curious about whether or not making me scream was anywhere on the lesson plan."

His body jolted, heat rushing through his veins. He looked over his shoulder at Sam, who was working steadily on something in the back of the shop. It was Anna's day off, so she wasn't on the property. But he and Sam were in the middle of a big custom job. A gate with a lot of intricate detail, with matching work for the deck and interior staircase of the home. Which meant they didn't get real time off right now.

"No," he returned, satisfied his brother wasn't paying attention, "that wasn't on the lesson plan. But I'm a big believer in improvisation."

"That was improvisation? In that case, it seems to be your strength."

The sarcasm he had expected. This innuendo, he had not. They'd both pulled away hard last night, no denying it. It would have been simple to go out and get more protection and neither of them had.

But damn, this new dynamic between them was a lot to get used to. Still, for all that it was kind of crazy, he knew what he wanted. "I'd like to show you more of my strengths tonight."

"You're welcome to improvise your way on over to my bed anytime." There was a pause. "Was that flirting? Was that *good* flirting?"

He laughed, tension exiting his body in a big gust. He should have known. He wasn't sure how he felt about this being part of the lesson. Not when he had been on the verge of initiating phone sex in the middle of a workday with his brother looming in the background. But keeping it part of the lesson was for the best. He didn't need to lose his head. This was Anna, after all. He was walking a very fine line here.

On the one hand, he knew keeping a clear line drawn in the sand was the right thing to do. They weren't just going to be able to slide right back into their normal relationship. Not after what had happened. On the other hand, Anna was…Anna. She was essential to him. And she wasn't jaded when it came to sexual relationships. Wasn't experienced. That meant he needed to handle her with care. And it would benefit him to remember that he couldn't play with her the way he did women with a little more experience. Women who understood that this was sex and nothing more.

It could never be meaningless sex with Anna. He couldn't have a meaningless conversation with her. That meant that whatever happened between them physically would change things, build things, tear things down. That was a fact. A scary one. Taking control, trying to harness it, label it, was the only solution he had. Otherwise, things would keep happening when they weren't prepared. That would be worse.

Maybe.

He cleared his throat. "Very good flirting. You got me all excited."

"Excellent," she said, sounding cheerful. "Also, I bought condoms."

He choked. "Did you?"

"They aren't ribbed. I wasn't sure if the one you used last night was."

"No," he said, rubbing the back of his neck and casting a side eye at his brother. "It wasn't."

"Good. I was looking for a repeat performance. I didn't want to get the wrong thing. Though maybe sometime we should try ribbed."

Sometime. Because there would be more than once.

More than last night. More than tonight. "We can try it if you want."

"I feel like we might as well try everything. I have a lot of catching up to do."

"Dancing," he said, trying to wage a battle with the heat that was threatening to take over his skull. "Do you want to go dancing tonight?"

"Not really. But I can see the benefit. Seeing as there will be dancing at the fund-raiser. And I bet I'm terrible at dancing."

"Great. I'm going to pick you up at seven. We're going to Ace's."

"Then I'll be ready."

He hung up the phone and suddenly realized he was at the center of Sam's keen focus. That bastard had been listening in the entire time. "Hot date tonight?" he asked.

"Dancing. With Anna," he said meaningfully. The meaning being *with Anna and not with you*.

"Well, then, you wouldn't mind if I tagged along." Jerkface was ignoring his meaning.

"I would mind."

"I thought this was just about some bet."

"It is," he lied.

"Uh-huh."

"You don't want to go out. You want to stay home and eat a TV dinner. You're just harassing me."

Sam shrugged. "I have to get my kicks somewhere."

"Get your own. Get laid."

"Nope."

"You're a weirdo."

"I'm selective."

Maybe Sam was, maybe he wasn't. Chase could honestly say that his brother's sex life was a mystery to him. Which was fine. Really, more than fine. Chase had a reputation,

Sam…did not. Well, unless that reputation centered around being grumpy and antisocial.

"Right. Well, you enjoy that. I'm going to go out."

"Chase," Sam said, his tone taking on a note of steel. "Don't hurt her."

Those words poked him right in the temper. "Really?"

"She's the best thing you have," Sam said, his voice serious. "You find a woman like that, you keep her. In whatever capacity you can."

"She's my best friend. I'm not going to hurt her."

"Not on purpose."

"I don't think you're in any position to stand there and lecture me on interpersonal relationships, since you pretty much don't have any."

"I have you," Sam said.

"Right. I'm not sure that counts."

"I have Anna. But if you messed things up with her, I won't have her, either."

Chase frowned. "You don't have feelings for her, do you?" He would really hate to have to punch his brother in the face. But he would.

"No. Not like you mean. But I know her, and I care about her. And I know you."

"What does that mean?"

Sam pondered that for a second. "You're not her speed."

"I'm not trying to be." He was getting ready to punch his brother in the face anyway.

"I'm just saying."

"You're just saying," he muttered. "Go *just say* somewhere else. A guy whose only friends are his younger brother and that brother's friend maybe shouldn't stand there and make commentary on relationships."

"I'm quiet. I'm perceptive. As you mentioned, I am an artist."

"You can't pull that out when it suits you and put it away when it doesn't."

"Sure I can. Artists are temperamental."

"Stop beating around the bush. Say what you want to say."

Sam sighed. "If she offers you more than friendship, take it, dumbass."

"Why would you think that she would ever offer that? Why would you think that I want it?"

He felt defensive. And more than a little bit annoyed. "She will. I'm not blind. Actually, being antisocial has its benefits. It means that I get to sit back and watch other people interact. She likes you. She always has. And she's the kind of good… Chase, we don't get good like that. We don't deserve it."

"Gee. Thanks, Sam."

"I'm not trying to insult you. I'm just saying that she's better than either of us. Figure out how to make it work if she wants to."

Everything in Chase recoiled. "She doesn't want to. And neither do I." He turned away from Sam, heading toward the door.

"Are you sleeping with her yet?"

Chase froze. "That isn't any of your business."

"Right. You are."

"Still not your business."

"Chase, we both have a lot of crap to wade through. Which is pretty obvious. But if she's standing there willing to pull you out, I'm just saying you need to take her up on her offer."

"She has enough crap of her own that she's hip deep in, Sam. I don't need her taking on mine."

Sam rubbed his hand over his forehead. "Yeah, that's always the thing."

"Anyway, she doesn't want me. Not like that. I mean,

not forever. This is just a…physical thing." Which was way more information than his brother deserved.

"Keep telling yourself that if it helps you sleep at night."

"I sleep like a baby, Sam." He continued out the door, heading toward his truck. He had to get back to the house and get showered and dressed so that he could pick up Anna. And he was not going to think about anything his brother had said.

Anna didn't want forever with him.

That thought immobilized him, forced him to imagine a future with Anna, stretching on and on into the distance. Holding her, kissing her. Sleeping beside her every night and waking up with her every morning.

Seeing her grow round with his child.

He shut it down immediately. That was a fantasy. One he didn't want. One he couldn't have.

He would have Anna as a friend forever, but the "benefits" portion of their relationship was finite.

So, he would just enjoy this while it lasted.

Ten

She looked like a cliché. A really slutty one. She wasn't sure she cared. But in her very short denim skirt and plaid shirt knotted above the waistline she painted quite the picture.

One of a woman looking to get lucky.

"Well," she said to her reflection—her made-up reflection, compliments of her trip to the store in Tolowa today, as was everything else. "You *are* looking to get lucky."

Fair. That was fair.

She heard the sound of a truck engine and tires on the gravel in her short little driveway. She was renting a house in an older neighborhood in town—not right in the armpit of town where she'd grown up, but still sort of on the fringe—and the yard was a little bit...rustic.

She wondered if Chase would honk. Or if he would come to the door.

Him coming to the door would feel much more like a date. A real date.

A *date* date.

Oh, Lord, what were they doing?

She had flirted with him on the phone, and she'd enjoyed it. Had wanted—very much—to push him even harder. Trading innuendo with him was…well, it was a lot more fun than she'd imagined.

There was a heavy knock on the door and she squeaked, hopping a little bit before catching her breath. Then she grabbed her purse and started to walk to the entry, trying to calm her nerves. He'd come to the door. That felt like A Thing.

You're being crazy. Friends with benefits. Not boyfriend.

The word *boyfriend* made her stomach lurch, and she did her best to ignore it. She jerked the door open, watching his face intently for his response to her new look. And she was not disappointed.

"Damn," he said, leaning forward, resting his forearm on the doorjamb. "I didn't realize you would be showing up dressed as Country Girl from My Dirtiest Dreams."

She shouldn't feel flattered by that. But she positively glowed. "It seemed fair, since you're basically the centerfold of *Blacksmith Magazine*."

He laughed. "Really? How would that photo shoot go?"

"You posing strategically in front of the forge with a bellows over your junk."

"I am not getting my *junk* near the forge. The last thing I need is sensitive body parts going up in flames."

"I know I don't want them going up in flames." She cleared her throat, suddenly aware of a thick blanket of awkwardness settling over them. She didn't know what to do with him now. Did she…not touch him unless they were going to have sex? Did she kiss him if she wanted to or did she need permission?

She needed a friends-with-benefits handbook.

"Um," she began, rather unsuccessfully. "What exactly are my benefits?"

"Meaning?"

"My benefits additional to this friendship. Do I...kiss you when I see you? Or..."

"Do you want to kiss me?"

She looked up at him, all sexy and delicious looking in his tight black T-shirt, cowboy hat and late-in-the-day stubble. "Is that a trick question? Because the only answer to 'Do I want to kiss a very hot guy?' is yes. But not if you don't want to kiss me."

He wrapped his arm around her waist, drawing her up against him before bending down to kiss her slowly, thoroughly. "Does that help?"

She let out a long, slow breath, the tension that had been strangling her since he'd arrived at her house leaving her body slowly. "Yes," she said, sighing. "It does."

"All right," he said, extending his hand. "Let's go."

She took hold of his hand, the warmth of his touch flooding her, making her stomach flip. She let him lead her to the truck, open her door for her. All manner of date-type stuff. The additional benefits were getting bound up in the dating lessons and at the moment she wasn't sure what was for her and what was for the Making Her Datable mission.

Then she decided it didn't matter.

She just clung to the good feelings the whole drive to Ace's.

When they got there, she felt the true weight of the spectacle they were creating in the community. Beaches was one thing. Them being together there had certainly caused a ripple. But everyone in Copper Ridge hung out at Ace's.

Sierra West, whose family was a client of both her and Chase, was in the corner with some other friends who were involved with local rodeo events. Sheriff Eli Garrett was over by the bar, along with his brother, Connor, and their wives, Sadie and Liss.

She looked the other direction and saw Holly and Ryan Masters sitting in the corner, looking ridiculously happy. Holly and Ryan had both grown up in foster care in Copper Ridge and so had been part of the town-charity-case section at school. Though Holly was younger and Ryan a little older, so she'd never been close friends with them. Behind them was Jonathan Bear, looking broody and unapproachable as usual.

She officially knew too many damn people.

"This town is the size of a postage stamp," she muttered as she followed Chase to a table where they could deposit their coats and her purse.

"That's good," he said. "Men are seeing you attached. It's all part of changing your reputation. That's what you want."

She grunted. "I guess." It didn't feel like what she wanted. She mostly just wanted to be alone with Chase now. No performance art required.

But she was currently a dancing monkey for all of Copper Ridge, so performance art was the order of the evening.

She also suddenly felt self-conscious about her wardrobe choice. Wearing this outfit for Chase hadn't seemed bad at all. Wearing it in front of everyone was a little much.

The jukebox was blaring, and Luke Bryan was demanding all the country girls shake it for him, so Anna figured—regardless of how comfortable she was feeling—it was as good a time as any for them to get out on the dance floor.

The music was fast, so people weren't touching. They were just sort of, well, *shaking it* near each other.

She was just standing there, looking at him and not shaking it, because she didn't know what to do next. It felt weird to be here in front of everyone in a skirt. It felt weird to be dancing with Chase. It felt weird to not touch him. But it would be weirder to touch him.

Hell if she knew what she was doing here.

Then he reached out, brushing his fingers down her arm. That touch, that connection, rooted her to the earth. To the moment. To him. Suddenly, it didn't matter so much what other people around them were doing. She moved in slightly, and he put his hand on her hip.

Then, before she was ready, the song ended, slowing things down. And now she really didn't know what to do. It seemed that Chase did, though. He wrapped his arm around her waist, drawing her in close, taking hold of her hand with his free one.

Her heart was pounding hard. And she was pretty sure her face was bright red. She looked up at Chase, his expression unreadable. He was not bright red. Of course he wasn't. Because even if this relationship was new for him, this kind of situation was not. He knew how to handle women. He knew how to handle sex feelings. Meanwhile, she was completely unsure of what to do. Like a buoy floating out in the middle of the ocean, just bobbing there on her own.

Her breathing got shorter, harder. Matching her heartbeat. She couldn't just dance with him like this. She needed to not be in front of people when she felt these things. She felt like her arousal was written all over her skin. Well, it was. She was blushing like a beacon. She could probably guide ships in from the sea.

She looked at Chase's face again. There was no way to tell what he was thinking. His dark gaze was shielded by the dim lighting, his jaw set, hard, his mouth in a firm line. That brief moment of connection that she'd felt was gone now. He was touching her still, but she had no idea what he was feeling.

She looked over to her left and noticed that people were

staring. Of course they were. She and Chase were dancing and that was different. And, of course, a great many of the stares were coming from women. Women who probably felt like they should be in her position. Like she didn't belong there.

And they could all see how much she wanted it. That she wanted him more than he wanted her. That she was the one who was completely and totally out of control. Needing him so much she couldn't even hide it.

And they all knew she didn't deserve it.

She pulled away from him, looking around, breathing hard. "I think... I just need a break."

She crossed the room and went back to their table, grabbing her purse and making her way over to the bar.

Chase joined her only a few moments later. "What's up?"

She shook her head. "Nothing."

"We were dancing, and then you freaked out."

"I don't like everybody watching us."

"That's the point, though."

That simple statement stabbed her straight through the heart. "Yeah. I know." That was the problem. He was so conscious of why they were doing this. This whole thing. And she could so easily forget. Could so easily let down all the walls and shields that she had put in place to protect her heart. And just let herself want.

She hated that. Hated craving things she couldn't have. Affection she could never hope to earn.

Her mother had left. And no amount of wishing that she would come back, no amount of crying over that lost love, would do anything to fix it. No amount of hoping her father would drop that crusty exterior and give her a hug when she needed it would make it happen. So she just didn't want. Or at least, she never let people see how much she wanted.

"I know," she said, her tone a little bit stiffer than she would like.

She was bombing out here. Failing completely at remaining cool, calm and unaffected. She was standing here in public, hemorrhaging needs all over the place.

"What's wrong?"

"I need a drink."

"Why don't we leave?"

She blinked. "Just...leave?"

"If you aren't having fun, then there's no point. Let's go."

"Where are we going?"

He grabbed her hand and started to lead her through the bar. "Somewhere fun."

She followed him out into the night, laughing helplessly when they climbed into the truck. "People are going to talk. That was all a little weird."

"Let them talk. They need something to do."

He started the engine and backed out of the parking lot, turning sharply and heading down the road, out of town.

"Where are we going?"

"Somewhere I bet you've never been."

"You don't know my life, Chase McCormack. You don't know where I've been."

"I do know your life, Anna Brown."

She gritted her teeth, because, of course, he did. She said nothing as they continued to drive up the road. And still said nothing when he turned onto a dirt road that forked into a narrower dirt road as it went up the mountain.

"What are we doing?" she asked again.

Just then, they came to a flat, clear area. She couldn't see anything; there were no lights except for the headlights on the truck, illuminating nothing but the side of another mountain, thick with evergreens.

"I want to make out with you. This is where you go do that."

"We're adults," she said, ignoring the giddy fluttering in her stomach. "We have our own bedrooms. And beds. We don't need to go make out in a car."

"*Need* is not the operative word here. We're expanding experiences and stuff." He flicked the radio on, country music filling the cab of the truck. "Actually, I think before we make out—" he opened the driver's-side door "—we should dance."

Now there was nobody here. Which meant there was no excuse. Actually, this made her a lot more emotional. She did not like that. She didn't like the superpower that Chase seemed to have of reaching down inside of her, past all the defenses, and grabbing hold of tender, emotional things.

But she wasn't going to refuse, either.

It was dark out here. At least there was that.

Before she had a chance to move, Chase was at her side of the truck, opening her door. He extended his hand. "Dance with me?"

She was having a strange out-of-body experience. She wasn't sure who this woman was, up in the woods with only a gorgeous man for company. A man who wanted to dance with her. A man who wanted to make out with her.

She unbuckled, accepting his offered hand and popping out of the truck. He spun her over to the front of the vehicle, the headlights serving as spotlights as the music played over the radio. "I'm kind of a crappy dancer," he said, pulling her in close.

"You don't seem like a crappy dancer to me."

"How many men have you danced with?"

She laughed. "Um, counting now?"

"Yeah."

"One."

He chuckled, his breath fanning over her cheekbone.

So intimate to share the air with him like this. Shocking. "Well, then, you don't have much to compare it to."

"I guess not. But I don't think I would compare either way."

"Oh, yeah? Why is that?"

"You're in a league of your own, Chase McCormack, don't you know?"

"Hmm. I have heard that a time or two. When teachers told me I was a unique sort of devil, sent there to make their lives miserable. Or all the times I used to get into it with my old man."

"Well, you did raise a lot of hell."

"Yeah. I did. I continue to raise hell, in some fashion. But I need people to see a different side of me," he said, drawing her even tighter up against him. "I need for them to see that Sam and I can handle our business. That we can make the McCormack name big again."

"Can you?" she asked, tilting her head up, her lips brushing his chin. The stubble there was prickly, masculine. Irresistible. So she bit him. Just lightly. Scraping her teeth over his skin.

He gripped her hair, pulling her head back. The sudden rush of danger in the movements sending a shot of adrenaline through her blood. This was so strange. Being in his arms and feeling like she was home. Like he was everything comforting and familiar. A warm blanket, a hot chocolate and a musical she'd seen a hundred times.

Then things would shift, and he would become something else entirely. A stranger. Sex, sin and all the things she'd never taken the time to explore. She liked that, too.

She was starting to get addicted to both.

"Oh, I can handle myself just fine," he said, his tone hard.

"Can you handle me?" she asked.

He slid his hand down to cup her ass, his eyes never

leaving hers as they swayed to the music. "I can handle you. However you want it."

"Hard," she said, her throat going dry, her words slightly unsteady. She wasn't sure what had possessed her to say that.

"You want it hard?" he asked, his words sounding strangled.

"Yes," she said.

"How else do you want it?" he asked, holding her against him, moving in time with the beat. She could feel his cock getting hard against her hip.

"Aren't you the one with the lesson plan?"

"You're the one in need of the education," he said.

"I don't want tonight to be about that," she said, and she was as sure about that as she'd been about wanting it hard and equally unsure about how she knew it.

"What do you want it to be about?"

"You," she said, tracing the sharp line of his jaw. "Me. That's about it."

"What do you want from me?" he asked.

Only everything. She shied away from that thought. "Show me what the fuss is about."

"I did that already."

Something hot and possessive spiked in her blood. Something she never could have anticipated, because she hadn't even realized that it lived inside of her. "No. Something you don't give other women, Chase. You're my friend. You're...more to me than one night and an orgasm. You're right. I could have gotten that from a lot of guys. Well, maybe not the orgasm. But sex for sure. My coveralls aren't that much of a turnoff. And you could have any woman. So give me you. And I'll give you me. Don't hold back."

"You're...not very experienced."

She stretched up on tiptoes, pressing her lips to his. "Did I ask for a gentleman? Or did I ask for hard?"

He tightened his grip on her hair, and this time when she looked up at his face, she didn't see a stranger. She saw Chase. The man. The whole man. Not divided up into parts. Not Her Friend Chase or Her Lover Chase, but just…Chase.

He was all of these things. Fun and laid-back, intense and deeply sexual. She wanted it all. She craved it all. As hard as he could. As much as he could. And still, it would never, ever be enough.

"Go ahead," she said, "take me, cowboy."

She didn't have to ask twice.

He propelled them both backward, pressing her up against the truck, kissing her deeply, a no-holds-barred possession of her mouth. She hadn't even realized kissing like this existed. She wasn't entirely sure what she had thought kissing was for. Affection. A prelude to sex. This was something else entirely. This was a language all its own. Words that didn't exist in English. Words that she knew Chase would never be able to say.

And her body knew that. Understood it. Responded. As surely as it would have if he had spoken.

She was drowning. In this, in him. She hadn't expected emotion to be this…fierce. She hadn't really expected emotion at all. She hadn't understood. She really had not understood.

But then she didn't have the time to think about it. Or the brainpower. He tugged on her hair, drawing her head to the side before he pressed his lips to her tender neck, his teeth scraping along the sensitive skin before he closed his lips around her and sucked hard.

"You want it hard?" he asked, his voice rough. "Then we're going to do it my way."

He grabbed hold of her hips, turning her so that she

was facing the truck. "Scoot just a little bit." He guided her down to where the cab of the truck ended and the bed began. "Grab on." She curved her fingers around the cold metal, a shiver running down her spine. "You ever do it like this?" he asked.

She laughed, more because she was nervous than because she thought the question was funny. "Chase, before you I had never even given a guy a blow job. Do you think I've ever done this before?"

"Good," he said, his tone hard, very definitely him. "I like that. I'm a sick bastard. I like the fact that no other man has ever done this to you before. I should feel guilty." He reached around and undid the top button on her top. "But I'm just enjoying corrupting you."

He undid another button, then another. She wasn't wearing a bra underneath the top. Because, frankly, when you were as underendowed as she was, there really wasn't any point. Also, it made things a little bit more easy access. Though that wasn't something she had thought about until just now. Until Chase undid the last button and left her completely bare to the cool night air.

"I'm kind of enjoying being corrupted."

"I didn't tell you you could talk."

She shut her mouth, surprised at the commanding tone he was taking. Not entirely displeased about it. He cupped her breasts, squeezing them gently before moving his hands down her stomach, bringing them around her hips. Then he tugged her skirt down, leaving her in nothing but her boots and her underwear.

"We'll leave the boots on. I wouldn't want you to step on anything sharp."

She didn't say anything. She bit her lip, eagerly anticipating what he might do next. He slipped his hand down between her thighs, his fingertips edging beneath her panties. He stroked his fingers through her folds, a harsh growl escaping his lips. "You're wet for me," he said—not a question.

She nodded, closing her eyes, trying to keep from hurtling over the edge as soon as his fingertips brushed over her. But it was a pretty difficult battle she was waging. Just the thought of being with Chase again was enough to take her to the precipice. His touch nearly pushed her over immediately.

He gripped her tightly with his other hand, drawing her ass back up against his cock as he teased her between her legs with his clever fingers. He slipped one deep inside of her, continuing to toy with her with the edge of his thumb while he thrust in and out of her slowly. He added a second finger, then another. And she was shaking. Trembling with the effort of holding back her climax.

But she didn't want it to end like this. Didn't want it to end so quickly. Mostly, she just didn't want him to know that with one flick of his fingertip over her sensitized flesh he could make her come so hard she wouldn't be able to see straight. Because at the end of the day it didn't matter how much she wanted him; she still had her pride. She still rebelled against the idea of revealing herself quite so easily.

She probably already had. Here she was, mostly naked, out underneath the stars. Here she was, telling him she wanted just the two of them, that she wanted it hard. Probably there were no secrets left. Not really. There were all sorts of unspoken truths filling in the silences between them, but she felt like they were easy enough to read, if he wanted to look at them.

He might not. She didn't really want to. Yet it didn't make them go away.

But she could ignore them. She could focus on this. On his touch. On the dark magic he was working on her body, the spell that was taking her over completely.

He swept her hair to the side, pressing a hot kiss to the

back of her neck. And then there was no holding back. Climax washed over her like a wave as she shuddered out her release.

"Good girl," he whispered, kissing her again before moving away for a moment. He pushed her panties down her legs, helping her step out of them, then he kissed her thigh before straightening.

She heard him moving behind her. But she didn't change her position. She stood there, gripping the back of the truck. Dimly, she was aware the radio was still on. That they had a sound track to this illicit encounter in the woods. It added to the surreal, out-of-body quality.

But then he was back with her, touching her, kissing her, and it didn't feel so surreal anymore. It was too raw. Too real. His voice, his scent, his touch. He was there. There was no denying it. This wasn't fantasy. Fantasy was gauzy, distant. This was sharp, so sharp she was afraid it would cut right into her. Dangerous. She wanted it. All of it. And she was afraid that in the end there would be nothing of her left. At least nothing that she recognized. That his friendship wouldn't be something that she recognized. But they'd gone too far to turn back, and she didn't even want to anymore. She wanted to see what was on the other side of this. Needed to see what was on the other side.

He reached up, bracing his hand on the back of her neck, holding her hip with the other as he positioned himself at the entrance to her body. He pressed the blunt head of his erection against her, sliding in easily, thrusting hard up inside her. She gasped as he went deeper than he had before. This was almost overwhelming. But she needed it. Embraced it.

His hold was possessive, all-encompassing. She felt like she was being consumed by him completely. By her desire for him. Warmth bloomed from where he held her, bled down beneath the surface of her skin, hemorrhaged in her chest.

"I fantasized about this," he said, the words seeming to scrape along his throat. Rough, raw. "Holding you like this. Holding on to your hips as I did this to you."

She couldn't respond. She couldn't say anything. His words had grabbed ahold of her, squeezing her throat tight, making it impossible for her to speak. He had fantasized about her. About this.

This position should feel less personal. More distant. But it didn't. That made it… It made it exactly what she had asked for. This was for her. And this was him. What he wanted, not just the next item on a list of things she needed to learn. Not just a set routine that he had with women he slept with.

He slid his hand down along the line of her spine, pressing firmly, the impression of his possession lingering on her skin. Then he held both of her hips tight, his blunt fingertips digging into her skin. He thrust harder into her, his skin slapping against hers, the sound echoing in the darkness. She gripped the truck hard, lowering her head, a moan escaping her lips.

"You wanted hard, baby," he ground out. "I'll give it to you hard."

"Yes," she whispered.

"Who are you saying yes to?" There was an edge to his words, a desperation she hadn't imagined he would feel, not with her. Not over this.

"Chase," she said, closing her eyes tight. "Yes, Chase. Please. I need this. I need you."

She needed all of him. And she suddenly realized why those thoughts about having someone to spend her nights with had seemed wrong. Because at the end of the day when she thought of sharing evenings with someone, when she thought of curling up under a blanket with someone, of watching *Oklahoma!* with someone for the hundredth time, it was Chase. It was always Chase. And that meant no other man had ever been able to get close enough to her. Because he was the fantasy. And as long as he was the fantasy, no one else had a place.

And now, now after this, she was ruined forever. Because she would never be able to do this with another man. Ever. It would always be Chase's hand she imagined on her skin. That firm grip of his that she craved.

He flexed his hips, going harder into her, then slipped his fingers around between her thighs again, stroking her as he continued to fill her. Then he leaned forward, biting her neck as he slammed into her one last time, sending them both over the edge. He growled, pulsing inside of her as he found his release. The pain from his teeth mingled with the all-consuming pleasure rolling through her in never-ending waves, pounding over her so hard she didn't think it would ever end. She didn't think she could survive it.

And when it passed, it was Chase who held her in his arms.

There was no denying it. No escaping it. And she was scraped raw. As stripped as she'd been after their first encounter, she was even more exposed now. Because she had read into all those empty, unspoken things. Because she had finally realized what everything meant.

Her asking him for help. Her kissing him. Her going down on him.

Her not having another man in her life in any capacity.

It was because she wanted Chase. All of Chase. It was why everything had come together for her tonight. Why she'd realized she couldn't compartmentalize him.

She wasn't ready to think the words yet, though. She couldn't. She did her very best to hold them at bay. To stop herself from thinking the things that would crumble her defenses once and for all.

Instead, she released her hold on the truck and turned to face him, looping her arms around his neck, pressing her bare body against his, luxuriating in him.

"That was quite the dance lesson," she said finally.

"A lot more fun than it would have been in Ace's." He slid his hand down to her butt, holding her casually. She loved that. So much more than she should.

"Yeah, we would have gotten thrown out for that."

"But can you imagine the rumors?"

"Are they really rumors if everyone has actually seen you screw?"

"Good question," he said, leaning forward and nipping her lower lip.

"You're bitey," she said.

"And you like to be bitten."

She couldn't deny it. "I guess I should… I mean, I have to work tomorrow."

"Me, too," he said, sounding regretful.

She wanted so badly to ask him to stay with her. But he wasn't bringing it up. And she didn't know if the almighty Chase McCormack actually *slept* with the women he was sleeping with.

So she didn't ask.

And when he dropped her off at her house, leaving her at her doorstep, she tried very, very hard not to regret that.

She didn't succeed.

Eleven

The best thing about having her own shop was working alone. Some people might find it lonely; Anna found it a great opportunity to run through every musical number she knew. She had already gone through the entirety of *Oklahoma!* and was working her way through *Seven Brides for Seven Brothers*.

Admittedly, she wasn't the best singer in the world, but in her own shop she was the best singer around.

And if the music helped drown out all of the neuroses that were scampering around inside of her, asking her to deal with her Chase feelings, then so much the better. She didn't want to deal with Chase feelings.

"When you're in love, when you're in love, there is no way on earth to hide it," she sang operatically, the words echoing off the walls.

She snapped her mouth shut. That was a bad song. A very bad song for this moment. She was not… She just wasn't going to think about it.

She turned her focus back to the tractor engine she currently had in a million little pieces. At least an engine was concrete. A puzzle she could solve. It was tactile, and most of the time, if she could just get the right parts, find the source of the problem, she could fix it. That wasn't true with much of anything else in life. That was one reason she found a certain sort of calm in the garage.

Plus, it was something her father knew how to do. He was his own mechanic, and weekends were often spent laboring over his pickup truck, getting it in working order so that he could drive it to work Monday. So she had watched, she had helped. It was about the only way she had been able to connect with her gruff old man. It was still about the only way she could connect with him.

It certainly wasn't through musicals. It could never have been a desire to be seen differently by other kids at school. A need to look prettier for a boy that she liked.

So she had chosen carburetors.

"But it can't be carburetors forever." Well, it could be. In that she imagined she would do this sort of work for the rest of her life. She loved it. She was successful at it. She filled a niche in the community that needed to be filled. But…it couldn't be the only thing she was. She needed to do more than fill. She needed to…be filled.

And right now everything was all kind of turned on its head. Or bent over the back of a pickup truck. Her cheeks heated at the memory.

Yeah, Chase had definitely come by his reputation honestly. It wasn't difficult to see why women lost their everloving minds over him.

That made her frown. Because she didn't like to think that she was just one of the many women losing their minds over him because he had a hot ass and skilled hands. She had known about the hot ass for years. It hadn't made her lose her mind. In fact, she didn't really think she had lost her mind now. She knew exactly what she was doing. She frowned even more deeply.

Did she know what she was doing? They had stopped and had discussions, made conscious decisions to do this friends-with-benefits thing. Tricked themselves into thinking that they were in control of this. Or at least that's what she had been doing. But as she had been carried away on a wave of emotion last night, she had known for an absolute fact that she wasn't in control of any of this.

"Doesn't mean I'm going to stop."

That, at least, was the absolute truth. He would have to be the one to call it off.

Just the thought made her heart crumple up into a little ball.

"Quitting time yet?"

She turned to see Chase standing in the doorway. This was a routine she could get used to. She wanted to cross the space between them and kiss him. And why not? She wasn't hiding her attraction to him. They weren't hiding their association.

She dropped her ratchet, wiped her hands on her coveralls and took two quick steps, flinging herself into his arms and kissing him on the lips. She wasn't embarrassed until about midway through the kiss, when she realized she had been completely and totally enthusiastic and hadn't hidden any of it. But he was holding on to her, and he was kissing her back, so maybe it didn't matter. Maybe it was okay.

When they parted, he was smiling.

Her heart felt tender, exposed. But warm, like it was being bathed in sunlight. Something to do with that smile of his. With that easy acceptance of what she had offered. "I think it's about time to quit," she said.

"I like your look," he said, gesturing to her white tank top, completely smeared with grease and dirt, and her coveralls, which were unbuttoned and tied around her waist.

"Really?"

"Last night you were my dirty country girl fantasy and today you're a sexy mechanic fantasy. Do you take requests? Around Christmas you could go for Naughty Mrs. Claus."

She rolled her eyes, grabbing the end of her tank top and knotting it up just under her breasts. "Maybe more like this? Though I think I'm missing the breast implants."

His smile turned wicked. "Baby, you aren't missing a damn thing."

Her heart thundered harder, a rush of adrenaline flowing through her. "I didn't think this was your type. Remember? You had to give me a makeover."

"Yeah, that was stupid. I actually think I just needed to get knocked upside the head."

"Did I…knock you upside the head?"

"Yeah." He wrapped his arms around her bare waist, his fingertips playing over her skin. "You're pretty perfect the way you are. You never needed a dress or high heels. I mean, you're welcome to wear them if you want. I'm not going to complain about that outfit you wore last night. But all that stuff we talked about in the beginning, about you needing to change so that people would believe we were together… I guess everyone is just going to have to believe that I changed a little bit."

"Have you changed?" she asked, brushing her thumb over his lower lip. A little thrill skittered down her spine. That she could touch him like this. Be so close to him. Share this kind of intimacy with a man she had had a certain level of emotional intimacy with for years and years.

It was wonderful. It also made her ache. Made her feel like her insides were being broken apart with a chisel. And she was willingly submitting to it. She didn't know quite what was happening to her.

Are you sure you don't?

"Something did," he said, his dark eyes boring into hers.

"You know," she said, trying to tamp down the fluttering that was happening in her chest, "I think it's only fair that I give you a few lessons."

"What kind of lessons?" he asked, his gaze sharpening.

"I'm not sure you know your way around an engine quite the way you should," she said, smiling as she wiggled out of his hold.

"Oh, really?"

She nodded, grabbing hold of a rag and slinging it over her shoulder before picking up her ratchet again. "Really."

"Is this euphemistic engine talk?"

"Do you think I'm expressing dissatisfaction with the way you work under my hood?"

He chuckled. "You're really getting good at this flirting thing."

"I am. That was good. And dirty."

"I noticed." He moved behind her, sweeping her hair to the side and kissing her neck. "But if you're implying that I didn't do a very good job...I would have to clear my good name."

"I was talking about literal engines, Chase. But if you really want to try to up your game, I'm not going to stop you."

"What's that?" he asked, reaching past her and pointing to one of the parts that were spread out on the worktable in front of her.

"A cylinder head. I'm replacing that and the head gasket on the engine. And I had to take a lot of things apart to get to it."

"When do you need to have it done?"

"Not until tomorrow."

"So you don't need me to play the part of lovely assistant while you finish up tonight?"

"I would like you to assist me with a few things," she

said, planting her hand at the center of his chest and pushing him lightly. The backs of his knees butted up against the chair that was behind him and he sat down, looking up at her, a predatory smile curving his lips.

"Is this going to be a part of my lesson?"

"Yeah," she said, "I thought it might be."

Last night had been incredible. Last night, he had given her something that felt special. Personal. Now she wanted to give him something. To show him what was happening inside of her, because she could hardly bring herself to think it. She wanted... She just wanted. In ways that she hadn't allowed herself to want in a long time. More. Everything.

"What exactly are you going to teach me?"

"Well, I could teach you all the parts of the tractor engine. But we would be here all night. And it would just slow me down. Someday, we can trade. You can give me some welding secrets. Teach me how to pound steel."

"That sounds dirty, too."

"Lucky me," she said, stretching her arms up over her head, her shirt riding up a little higher. She knew what she wanted to do. But she also felt almost petrified. This was... well, this was the opposite of protecting herself. This was putting herself out there. Risking humiliation. Risking doing something wrong while revealing how desperately she wanted to get it right.

But she wanted to give him something. And honestly, there was no bigger gift she could give him than vulnerability. To show him just how much she wanted him.

She swayed her hips to the right, then moved them back toward the left in a slow circle. She watched his face, watched the tension in his jaw increase, the sharpness in his eyes get positively lethal. And that was all the encouragement she needed. She'd seen enough movies with lap dances that she had a vague idea of how this should go. Maybe her idea was the PG-13-rated version, but she could improvise.

He moved his hand over the outline of his erection, squeezing himself through the denim as she continued to move. Maybe it wasn't rhinestones and a miniskirt, but he didn't seem to mind her white tank top and coveralls. He was still watching her with avid interest as she untied the sleeves from around her waist and let the garment drop down around her feet. She kicked it off to the side, revealing her denim cutoff shorts underneath it.

"Come here," he said, his voice hard.

"I'm not taking orders from you. You have to be patient."

"I'm not feeling very patient, honey."

"What's my name?"

"Anna," he ground out. "Anna, I'm not feeling very patient."

"Not enough women have made you wait. You're getting spoiled."

She slid her hand up her midsection, her own fingertips combined with the electric look on Chase's face sending heat skittering along her veins. She let her fingers skim over her breast, gratified when his breath hissed through his teeth.

"Anna..."

"You know me pretty well, don't you? But you didn't know all this." She moved her hand back down, over her stomach, her belly button, sliding her fingers down beneath the waistband of her shorts, stroking herself where she was wet and aching for him. His fingers curled around the edge of the chair, his knuckles white, the cords on his neck standing out, the strength it was taking him to remain seated clear and incredibly compelling.

"Take them off," he said.

"Didn't I just tell you that you're not in charge?"

"Don't play games with me."

"Maybe patience is the lesson you need to learn."

"I damn well don't," he growled.

She turned around, facing away from him, taking a deep breath as she unsnapped her shorts and pushed them down her hips, revealing the other purchase she had made at the store yesterday. A black, lacy thong, quite unlike any other pair of underwear she had ever owned. And she had slipped it on this morning hoping that this would be the end of her day.

"Holy hell," he said.

She knew that she was not the first woman to take her clothes off for him. Much less the first woman to reveal sexy underwear. But that only made his appreciation for hers that much sweeter. She swayed her hips back and forth before dropping down low, and sweeping back up. It felt so cheesy, and at the same time she was pretty proud of herself for pulling it off.

When she turned to face him, his expression was positively feral.

Her shirt was still knotted beneath her breasts, and now she was wearing work boots, a thong and the top. If Chase thought the outfit was a little bit silly, he certainly didn't show it.

She moved over to the chair, straddling him, leaning in and kissing him on the lips. "I want you," she said.

She had said it before. But this was more. Deeper. This was the truth. Her truth, the truest thing inside of her. She wanted Chase. In every way. Forever. She swallowed hard, grabbing hold of his T-shirt and tugging it up over his head. She licked her lips, looking at his body, at his chest, speckled with just the right amount of dark hair, at his abs, so perfectly defined and tempting.

She reached between them, undoing his belt and jerking it through the loops, before tugging his pants and underwear down low on his hips. He put his hand on her backside, holding her steady as she maneuvered herself so that she was over him, rubbing up against his arousal. "I would never have considered doing something like this before last week. Not with anyone. It's just you," she said, leaning in and kissing his lips lightly. "You do this to me."

He shuddered beneath her, her words having the exact effect she hoped they would. He liked feeling special, too.

He took hold of her hand, drawing it between them, curving her fingers around him. "And you do this to me. You make me so hard, it hurts. I've never wanted a woman like this before. Ever."

She flexed her hips, squeezed him tighter, trapping him between her palm and the apex of her thighs. "Why? Why do you want me like this?"

It was important to know. Essential.

"Because it's you, Anna. There's this idea that having sex with a stranger is supposed to be exciting. Because it's dirty. Because it's wrong. Maybe because it's unknown? But I've done that. And this is… You're right. I know you. Knowing you like this… Your face is so familiar to me, your voice. Knowing what it looks like when I make you come, how you sound when I push you over the edge, baby, there's nothing hotter than that."

His words washed over her, everything she had never known she needed. This full, complete acceptance of who she was. Right here in her garage. The mechanic, the woman. The friend, the lover. He wanted her. And everything that meant.

She didn't even try to keep herself from feeling it now. Didn't try to keep herself from thinking it.

She loved him. So much. Every part of him, with every part of her. Her friend. The only man she really wanted. The only person she could imagine sharing her days and nights and blankets and musicals with.

And that realization didn't even make her want to pull

away from him. Didn't make her want to hide. Instead, she wanted to finish this. She wanted to feel connected to him. Now that she was in, she was in all the way. Ready to expose herself completely, scrape herself raw, all for him.

She rose up so that she was on her knees, tugged her panties down her hips and maneuvered herself so that she was able to dispense with them completely before settling over him, grabbing hold of his broad shoulders as she sank down onto his hardened length.

He swore, the harsh word echoing in the empty space. "Anna, I need to get a condom."

She pulled away from him quickly, hovering over him as he lifted his hips, grabbing his wallet and pulling out a condom with shaking hands, taking care of the practicalities quickly. She was trembling, both with the adrenaline rush that accompanied the stupidity of her mistake and with need. With regret because she wished that he was still inside of her even though it wouldn't be responsible at all.

Soon, he was guiding her back onto him, having protected them both. Thankfully, he was a little more with it than she was.

He gripped her tightly, guiding her movements at first, helping her establish a rhythm that worked for them both.

He moved his hands around, brushing his fingertips along the seam of her ass before teasing her right where their bodies were joined. She gasped, grabbing hold of the back of the chair, flexing her hips, chasing her own release as he continued to touch her. To push her higher.

She slid her hands up, cupping his face, holding him steady. She met his gaze, a thrill shooting down her spine. "Anna," he rasped, the words skating over her skin like a caress, touching her everywhere.

Pleasure gripped her, low and tight, sending her over the edge. She held his face as she shuddered out her orgasm and chanted his name, endlessly. Over and over again.

And when it was over, he held her to him, kissing her lips, whispering words against her mouth that she could barely understand. She didn't need to. The only words she understood were the ones she most needed to hear.

"Stay with me tonight."

Twelve

They dressed and drove across the property in Chase's truck. His heart was still hammering like crazy, and he had no idea what the hell he was doing. But then, it was Anna. She wasn't some random hookup. He wanted her again, and having her spend the night seemed like the best way to accomplish that.

He ignored the little terror claws that wrapped themselves around his heart and squeezed, and focused instead on the heavy sensation in his gut. In his dick. He wanted her, and dammit, he was going to have her.

The image of her dancing in front of him in the shop… that would haunt him forever. And it was his goal to collect a few more images that would make his life miserable when their physical relationship ended.

That was normal.

He parked the truck, then got out, following Anna mutely up the steps. When they got to the door, Anna paused.

"I don't…have anything with me. No porcupine pajamas."

Some of the tension in his chest eased. "You won't need pajamas in my bed," he said, his voice low, almost unrecognizable even to himself.

Which was fair enough, since this whole damn situation was unrecognizable. Saying this kind of stuff to Anna. Seeing her like this. Wanting her like this.

She was a constant. She was stability. And he felt shaky as hell right now.

"I've never spent the night with anyone," she blurted.

The words hit him hard in the chest. Along with the realization that this was a first for him, too. He knew it, logically. But for some reason it hadn't seemed momentous when he'd issued the invitation. Because it was Anna and sleeping with her had seemed like the most natural thing on earth. He liked talking to her, liked kissing her, liked having sex with her, and he didn't want her to leave. So the obvious choice was to ask her to stay the night.

Now it was hitting him, though. What that usually meant. Why he didn't do it.

But it was too late to take the invitation back, and anyway, he didn't know if he wanted to.

"I haven't, either," he said.

She blinked. "You…haven't? I mean, I had a ten-minute roll in the hay—literally—with a loser in high school, so I know why I've never spent the night with anyone. But you…you do this a lot."

"Are you calling me a slut?"

"Yes," she said, deadpan. "No judgment, but yeah, you're kind of slutty."

"Well, you don't have to spend the night with someone when you're done with them. I guess that's why I haven't. Because I am kind of slutty, and it has nothing to do with liking the person I'm with. Just…"

Oblivion. The easiest, most painless connection on earth with no risk involved whatsoever.

But he wasn't going to say that.

Anna wasn't oblivion. Being with her was like…being inside his own skin, really in it, and feeling it, for the first time since he was sixteen.

Like driving eighty miles per hour on the same winding road that had killed his parents, daring it to come for him, too. He'd felt alive then. Alive and pushing up against the edge of mortality as hard as he could.

Then he'd backed way off the gas. And he'd backed way off ever since.

This was the closest thing to tasting that surge of adrenaline, that rush he'd felt since the day he'd basically begged the road to take him, too.

You're a head case.

Yes, he was. But he'd always known that. Anna hadn't, though.

"Just?" she asked, eyebrows shooting up. She wasn't going to let that go, apparently.

"It's just sex."

"And what is this?" she asked, gesturing between the two of them.

"Friendship," he said honestly. "With some more to it."

"Those benefits."

"Yeah," he said. "Those."

He shoved his hands in his pockets, feeling like he'd just failed at something, and he couldn't quite figure out what. But his words were flat in the evening air. Just sort of dull and resting between them, wrong and weird, but he didn't know what to do about it.

Because he didn't know what else to say, either.

"Want to come inside?" he asked finally.

"That is where your bed is," she said.

"It is."

They made their way to the bedroom, and somehow it all felt different. He could easily remember when she'd been up here just last week, walking in those heels and that dress. When he'd been overwhelmed with the need to touch her, but wouldn't allow himself to do so.

He could also remember being in here with her plenty of times before. Innocuous as sharing the space with any friend.

How? How had they ever existed in silences that weren't loaded? In moments that weren't wrapped in tension. In isolation that didn't present the very tempting possibility of chasing pleasure together. Again and again.

This wasn't friendship plus benefits. That implied the friendship remained untouched and the benefits were an add-on. Easy to stick there, easy to remove. But that wasn't the case.

Everything was different. The air around them had changed. How the hell could he pretend the friendship was the same?

"I'm just—" She smiled sheepishly and pulled her shirt up over her head. "Sorry." Then she unhooked her bra, tossing it onto the floor. He hadn't had a chance to look at her breasts the last time they'd had sex. She'd kept them covered. Something that had added nicely to the tease back in the shop. But he was ready to drop to his knees and give thanks for their perfection now.

"Why are you apologizing for flashing me?"

"Because. In the absence of pajamas I need to get comfortable now." She stripped her shorts off, and her underwear—those shocking black panties that he simply hadn't seen coming, much like the rest of her—and then she flopped down onto his bed. He didn't often bring women back here.

Sometimes, depending on the circumstances, but if they had a hotel room, or their own place available, that was his preference. So it was a pretty unusual sight in general. A naked woman in his room. Anna, in this familiar place—naked and warm and about as inviting as anything had ever been—was enough to make his head explode.

His head, and other places.

"You never have to apologize for being naked." He stripped his shirt off, then continued to follow her lead, until he was wearing nothing.

He lay down beside her, not touching her, just looking at her. This was hella weird. If a woman was naked, he was usually having sex with her, bottom line. He didn't lie next to one, simply looking at her. Right now, Anna was something like art and he just wanted to admire her. Well, that wasn't *all* he wanted. But it was what he wanted right now. To watch the soft lamplight cast a warm glow over her curves, to examine every dip and hollow on the map of her figure. To memorize the rosy color of her nipples, the dark hair at the apex of her thighs. The sweet flare of her hips and the slight roundness of her stomach. She was incredible. She was Anna. Right now, she was his.

That thought made his stomach tighten. How long had it been since something was his?

This place would always be McCormack, through and through. The foundation of the forge and the business… it was built on his great-grandfather's back, carried down by his grandfather, handed to their father.

And he and Sam carried it now.

This ranch would always be something they were bound to by blood, not by choice. Even if given the choice, he could probably never leave. Their family… It didn't feel like their family anymore. It hadn't for a lot of years.

It was two of them, him and Sam. Two of them trying so damn hard to push this legacy back to where it had been. To make their family extend beyond these walls, beyond these borders. To fulfill all of the promises he'd made to his dad, even though the old man had never actually heard them.

Even though Chase had made them too late.

And so there was something about that. Anna, this moment, being for him. Something that he chose, instead of something that he'd inherited.

"I like when you look at me like that," she said, her voice hushed.

"I like when you take control like you did back in the shop. I like seeing you realize how beautiful you are," he said. It was true. He was glad that she knew now. And pissed that she was going to take that knowledge and work her magic on some other man with her newfound power. He wanted to kill that man.

But he could never hope to take his place, so he wouldn't.

"You're the first person who has made me feel like it all fit. And maybe it's because you're my friend. Maybe it's because you know me," she said.

"I don't follow."

"I had to be tough," she said, her tone demonstrating just that. "All my life I've had to be tough. My brothers raised me, and they did a damn good job, and I know you think they're jerks, and honestly a lot of the time they are. But they were young boys who were put in charge of taking care of their kid sister. So they took care of me, but they tortured me in that way only brothers can. Probably because I tortured them in ways that most little sisters could never dream. They didn't go out in high school. They had to make sure I was taken care of. They didn't trust my dad to do it. He wasn't stable enough. He would go out to the bar and get drunk, and he would call needing a ride home. They handled things so that I didn't have to. And I never felt like I could make their lives more difficult by showing how hard it was for me."

She shifted, sighing heavily before she continued. "And

then there was my dad. He didn't know what to do with a daughter. As pissed as he was that his wife left, I think in some ways he was relieved, because he didn't have to figure out how to fit a woman into his life anymore. But then I kind of started becoming a woman. And he really didn't know what to do. So I learned how to work on cars. I learned how to talk about sports. I learned how to fit. Even though it pushed me right out of fitting when it came to school. When it came to making friends."

He knew these things about Anna. Knew them because he'd absorbed them by being in her house, being near her, for fifteen years. But he'd never heard her say them. There was something different about that.

"You've always fit with me, Anna," he said, his voice rough.

"I know. And even though we've never talked about this, I'm pretty sure somehow you knew all of it. You always have. Because you know me. And you accept me. Not very many people know about the musicals. Because it always embarrassed me. Kind of a girlie thing."

"I guess so," he said, the words feeling inadequate.

"Also, it was my thing. And…I never like anyone to know how much I care about things. I… My mom loved old musicals," she said, her voice soft. "Sometimes I wonder what it would be like to watch them with her."

"Anna…"

"I remember sneaking out of my room at night, seeing the TV flickering in the living room. She would be watching *The Sound of Music* or *Cinderella. Oklahoma!* of course. And I would just hang there in the hall. But I didn't want to interrupt. Because by the end of the day she was always out of patience, and I knew she didn't want any of the kids to talk to her. But it was kind of like watching them with her." Anna's eyes filled with tears. "But now I just wish I had. I wish I had gone in and sat next to her. I wish I had risked her being upset with me. I never got the chance. She left, and that was it. So, maybe she would've been mad at me, or maybe she wouldn't have let me watch them with her. But at least I would've had the answer. Now I just wonder. I just remember that space between us. Me hiding in the hall, and her sitting on the couch. She never knew I was there. Maybe if I'd done a better job of connecting with her, she wouldn't have left."

"That's not true, Anna."

"She didn't have anyone to watch the movies with, Chase. And my dad was so… I doubt he ever gave her a damn scrap of tenderness. But maybe I could have. I think… I think that's what I was always trying to do with my dad. To make up for that. It was too late to make her stay, but I thought maybe I could hang on to him."

Chase tried to breathe past the tightness in his chest, but it was nearly impossible. "Anna," he said, "any parent that chooses to leave their child…the issue is with them. It was your parents' marriage. It was your mom. I don't know. But it was never you. It wasn't you not watching a movie with her, or irritating her, or making her angry. There was never anything you could do."

She nodded, a tear tracking down her pale cheek. "I do know that."

"But you still beat yourself up for it."

"Of course I do."

He didn't have a response to that. She said it so matter-of-factly, as though there was nothing else but to blame herself, even if it made no sense. He had no response because he understood. Because he knew what it was like to twist a tragedy in a thousand different ways to figure out how you could take it on yourself. He knew what it was like to live your life with a gaping hole where someone you loved should be. To try to figure out how you could have stopped the loss from happening.

In the years since his parents' accident he had moved beyond blame. Not because he was stronger than Anna, just because you could only twist death in so many different directions. It was final. And it didn't ask you. It just was. Blaming himself would have been a step too far into martyrdom.

Still, he knew about lingering scars and responses to those scars that didn't make much sense.

But he didn't know what it was like to have a parent choose to leave you. God knew his parents never would have chosen to abandon their sons.

As if she'd read his mind, Anna continued. "She's still out there. I mean, as far as I know. She could have come back. Anytime. I just feel like if I had given her even a small thing…well, then, maybe she would have missed me enough at some point. If she'd had anything back here waiting for her, she could have called. Just once."

"You were you," he said. "If that wasn't enough for her…fuck her."

She laughed and wiped another tear from her face. Then she shifted, moving closer to him. "I appreciate that." She paused for a moment, kissing his shoulder, then she continued. "It's amazing. I've never told you that before. I've never told anyone that before. It's just kind of crazy that we could know each other for so long and…there's still more we don't know."

He wanted to tell her then. About the day his parents died. About the complete and total hole it had torn in his life. She knew to a degree. They had been friends when it happened. He had been sixteen, and Sam had been eighteen, and the loss of everything they knew had hit so hard and fast that it had taken them out at the knees.

He wanted to tell her about his nightmares. Wanted to tell her about the last conversation he'd had with his dad.

But he didn't.

"Amazing" was all he said instead.

Then he leaned over and kissed her, because he couldn't think of anything else to do, couldn't think of anything else to say.

Liar.

A thousand things he wanted to tell her swirled around inside of him. A thousand different things she didn't know. That he had never told anybody. But he didn't want to open himself up like that. He just… He just couldn't.

So instead, he kissed her, because that he could do. Because of all the changes that existed between them, that was the one he was most comfortable with. Holding her, touching her. Everything else was too big, too unknown to unpack. He couldn't do it. Didn't want to do it.

But he wanted to kiss her. Wanted to run his hands over her bare curves. So he did.

He touched her, tasted her, made her scream. Because of all the things that were happening in his life, that felt right.

This was…well, it was a detour. The best one he'd ever taken, but a detour all the same. He was building the family business, like he had promised his dad he would do. Or like he should have promised him when he'd had the chance. He might never have been able to tell the old man to his face, but he'd promised it to his grave. A hundred times, a thousand times since he'd died.

That was what he had to do. That was on the other side of making love with Anna. Going to that benefit with her all dressed up, trying to help her get the kind of reputation she wanted. To send her off with all her newfound skills so that she could be with another man after.

To knuckle down and take the McCormack family ranch back to where it had been. Beyond. To make sure that Sam used his talents, to make sure that the forge and all the work their father had done to build the business didn't go to waste.

To prove that the fight he'd had with his father right before he died was all angry words and teenage bluster. That what he'd said to his old man wasn't real.

He didn't hate the ranch. He didn't hate the business. He didn't hate their name. He was their name, and damn him for being too young and stupid to see it then.

He was proving it now by pouring all of his blood, all of his sweat, all of his tears into it. By taking the little bit of business acumen he had once imagined might get him out of Copper Ridge and applying it to this place. To try to make it something bigger, something better. To honor all the work their parents had invested all those years.

To finish what they started.

He might not have ever made a commitment to a woman, but this ranch, McCormack Iron Works...was his life. That was forever.

It was the only forever he would ever have.

He closed those thoughts out, shut them down completely and focused on Anna. On the sweet scent of her as he lowered his head between her thighs and lapped at her, on the feel of her tight channel pulsing around his fingers as he stroked them in and out. And finally, on the tight, wet clasp of her around him as he slid home.

Home. That's really what it was.

In a way that nowhere else had ever been. The ranch was a memorial to people long dead. A monument that he would spend the rest of his life building.

But she was home. She was his.

If he let her, she could become everything.

No.

That denial echoed in his mind, pushed against him as he continued to pound into her, hard, deep, seeking the oblivion that he had always associated with sex before her. But it wasn't there. Instead, it was like a veil had been torn away and he could see all of his life, spreading out before him. Like he was standing on a ridge high in the mountains, able to survey everything. The past, the present, the future. So clear, so sharp it almost didn't seem real.

Anna was in all of it. A part of everything.

And if she was ever taken away...

He closed his eyes, shutting out that thought, a wave of pleasure rolling over him, drowning out everything. He threw himself in. Harder than he ever had. Grateful as hell that Anna had found her own release, because he'd been too wrapped up in himself to consider her first.

Then he wrapped his arms around her, wrapped her up against him. Wrapped himself up in her. And he pushed every thought out of his mind and focused on the feeling of her body against his, the scent of her skin. Feminine and sweet with a faint trace of hay and engine grease.

No other woman smelled like Anna.

He pressed his face against her breasts and she sighed, a sound he didn't think he'd ever get tired of. He let everything go blank. Because there was nothing in his past, or his future, that was as good as this.

Thirteen

Chase woke in a cold sweat, his heart pounding so heavily he thought it would burst through his bone and flesh and straight out into the open. His bed was empty. He sat up, rubbing his hand over his face, then forking his fingers through his hair.

It felt wrong to have the bed empty. After spending only one night wrapped around Anna, it already felt wrong. Not having her... Waking up in the morning to find that she wasn't there was... He hated it. It was unsettling. It reminded him of the holes that people left behind, of how devastating it was when you lost someone unexpectedly.

He banished the thought. She might still be here. But then, she didn't have any clean clothes or anything, so if she had gone home, he couldn't necessarily blame her. He went straight into the bathroom, took a shower, took care of all other morning practicalities. He resisted the urge to look at his phone, to call Anna's phone or to go downstairs and see if maybe she was still around. He was going to get through all this, dammit, and he was not going to behave as though he were affected.

As though the past night had changed something fundamental, not just between them, but in him.

He scowled, throwing open the bedroom door and heading down the stairs.

He stopped dead when he saw her standing there in the kitchen. She was wearing his T-shirt, her long, slim legs bare. And he wondered if she was bare all the way up. His mouth dried, his heart squeezing tight.

She wasn't missing. She wasn't gone. She was cooking him breakfast. Like she belonged here. Like she belonged in his life. In his house. In his bed.

For one second it made him feel like he belonged. Like she'd been the missing piece to making this his, to making it more than McCormack.

He felt like he was standing in the middle of a dream. Standing there looking at somebody else's life. At some wild, potential scenario that in reality he would never get to have.

Right in front of him was everything. And in the same moment he saw that, he imagined the hole that would be left behind if it was ever taken away. If he ever believed in this, fully, completely. If he reached out and embraced her now, there would be no words for how empty his arms would feel if he ever lost her.

"Don't you have work?" he asked, leaning against the doorjamb.

She turned around and smiled, the kind of smile that lit him up inside, from his head, down his toes. He did his very best not to return the gesture. Did his best not to encourage it in any way.

And he cursed himself when the glow leached out of her face. "Good morning to you, too," she said.

"You didn't need to make breakfast."

"*Au contraire*. I was hungry. So breakfast was needed."

"You could've gone home."

"Yes, Grumpy-Pants, I could have. But I decided to stay here and make you food. Which seemed like an adequate thank-you for the multiple orgasms I received yesterday."

"Bacon? You're trying to pay for your orgasms with bacon?"

"It seemed like a good idea at the time." She crossed her arms beneath her breasts and revealed that she did not, in fact, have anything on beneath the shirt. "Bacon is a borderline orgasmic experience."

"I have work. I don't have time to eat breakfast."

"Maybe if you had gotten up at a decent hour."

"I don't need you to lecture me on my sleeping habits," he bit out. "Is there coffee?"

"It's like you don't know me at all." She crossed the room and lifted a thermos off the counter. "I didn't want to leave it sitting on the burner. That makes it taste gross."

"I don't really care how it tastes. That's not the point."

She rested her hand on the counter, then rapped her knuckles against the surface. "What's going on?"

"Nothing."

"Stop it, Chase. Maybe you can BS the other bimbos that you sleep with, but you can't do it to me. I know you too well. This has nothing to do with waking up late."

"This is a bad idea," he said.

"What's a bad idea? Eating bacon and drinking coffee with one of your oldest friends?"

"Sleeping with one of my oldest friends. It was stupid. We never should've done it."

She just stood there, her expression growing waxen, and as the color drained from her face, he felt something even more critical being scraped from his chest, like he was being hollowed out.

"It's a little late for that," she pointed out.

"Well, it isn't too late to start over."

"Chase…"

"It was fun. But, honestly, we accomplished everything we needed to. There's no reason to get dramatic about it. We agreed that we weren't going to let it affect our friendship. And it…it just isn't working for me."

"It was working fine for you last night."

"Well, that was last night, Anna. Don't be so needy."

She drew back as though she had been slapped and he wanted to punch his own face for saying such a thing. For hitting her where he knew it would hurt. And he waited. Waited for her to grow prickly. For her to retreat behind the walls. For her to get angry and start insulting him. For her to end all of this in fire and brimstone as she scorched the earth in an attempt to disguise the naked pain that was radiating from her right now.

He knew she would. Because that was how it went. If he pushed far enough, then she would retreat.

She closed the distance between them, cupping his face, meeting his eyes directly. And he waited for the blow. "But I feel needy. So what am I going to do about that?"

He couldn't have been more shocked than if she had reached up and slapped him. "What?"

"I'm needy. Or maybe…wanty? I'm both." She took a deep breath. "Yes, I'm both. I want more. Not less. And this is… This is the moment where we make decisions, right? Well, I've decided that I want to move forward with this. I don't want to go back. I can't go back."

"Anna," he said, her name scraping his throat raw.

"Chase," she said, her own voice a whisper in response.

"We can't do this," he said.

He needed the Anna he knew to come to his rescue now. To laugh it all off. To break this tension. To say that it didn't matter. To wave her hand and say it was all whatever and they could forget it. But she wasn't doing that.

She was looking at him, her green eyes completely earnest, vulnerability radiating from her face. "We need to do this. Because I love you."

Anna could tell that her words had completely stunned Chase. Fair enough, they had shocked her just as much. She didn't know where all of this was coming from. This strength. This bravery.

Except that last night's conversation kept echoing in her mind. When she had told him about her mother. When she had told him about how she always regretted not closing the distance between them. Always regretted not taking the chance.

That was the story of her entire life. She had, from the time she was a child, refused to make herself vulnerable. Refused to open herself up to injury. To pain. So she pretended she didn't care. She pretended nothing mattered. She did that every time her father ignored her, every time he forgot an important milestone in her life. She had done it the first time she'd ever had sex with a guy and it had made her feel something. Rather than copping to that, rather than dealing with it, she had mocked him.

All of her inner workings were a series of walls and shields, carefully designed to keep the world from hitting the terrible, needy things inside of her. Designed to keep herself from realizing they were there. But she couldn't do it anymore. She didn't want to do it anymore. Not with Chase. She didn't want to look back and wonder what could have been.

She wanted more. She needed more. Pride be damned.

"I do," she said, nodding. "I love you."

"You can't."

"I'm pretty sure I can. Since I do."

"No," he said, the word almost desperate.

"No, Chase, I really do. I mean, I have loved you since

I was fifteen years old. And intermittently thought you were hot. But mostly, I just loved you. You've been my friend, my best friend. I needed you. You've been my emotional support for a long time. We do that for each other. But things changed in the past few days. You're my…everything." Her voice broke on that last word. "This isn't sex and friendship, it isn't two different things, this is all the things, combined together to make something so big that it fills me completely. And I don't have room inside my chest for shields and protection anymore. Not when all that I am just loves you."

"I can't do this," he bit out, stepping away from her.

"I didn't ask if you could do this. This isn't about you, not right now. Yes, I would like you to love me, too, but right now this is just about me saying that I love you. Telling you. Because I don't ever want to look back and think that maybe you didn't know. That maybe if I had said something, it could have been different." She swallowed hard, battling tears. "I don't know what's wrong with me. Unless it's a movie, I almost never cry, but you're making me cry a lot lately."

"I'm only going to make you cry more," he said. "Because I don't know how to do this. I don't know how to love somebody."

"Bull. You've loved me perfectly, just the way I needed you to for fifteen years. The way that you take care of this place, the way that you care for Sam… Don't tell me that you can't love."

"Not this kind. Not this… Not this."

"I'm closing the gap," she said, pressing on, even though she could see that this was a losing battle. She was charging in anyway, sword held high, chest exposed. She was giving it her all, fighting even though she knew she wasn't going to walk away unscathed. "I'm not going to wonder what would've happened if I'd just been brave enough to do it. I would rather cut myself open and bleed out. I would rather risk my heart than wonder. So I'm just going to say it. Stop being such a coward and love me."

He took another step back from her and she felt that gap she was so desperate to close widening. Watched as her greatest fear started to play out right before her eyes. "I just… I don't."

"You don't or you won't?"

"At the end of the day, the distinction doesn't really matter. The result is the same."

She felt like she was having an out-of-body experience. Like she was floating up above, watching herself get rejected. There was nothing she could do. She couldn't stop it. Couldn't change it. Couldn't shield herself.

It was…horrible. Gut-wrenching. Destructive. Freeing.

Like watching a tsunami racing to shore and deciding to surrender to the wave rather than fight it. Yeah, it would hurt like hell. But it was a strange, quiet space. Past fear, past hope. All she could hear was the sound of her heart beating.

"I'm going to go," she said, turning away from him. "You can have the bacon."

She had been willing to risk herself, but she wouldn't stand there and fall apart in front of him. She would fall apart, but dammit, it would be on her own time.

"Stay and eat," he said.

She shook her head. "No. I can't stay."

"Are we going to… Are we going to go to the gala together still?"

"No!" She nearly shouted the word. "We are not going to go together. I need to… I need to think. I need to figure this out. But I don't think things can be the same anymore."

It was his turn to close the distance between them. He grabbed hold of her arms, drawing her toward him, his expression fierce. "That was not part of the deal. It was friends plus benefits, remember? And then in the end we could just stop with the benefits and go back to the friendship."

"We can't," she said, tears falling down her cheeks. "I'm sorry. But we can't."

"What the hell?" he ground out.

"We can't because I'm all in. I'm not going to sit back and pretend that it didn't really matter. I'm not going to go and hide these feelings. I'm not going to shrug and say it doesn't really matter if you love me or not. Because it does. It's everything. I have spent so many years not wanting. Not trying. Hiding how much I wanted to be accepted, hiding how desperately I wanted to try to look beautiful, how badly I wanted to be able to be both a mechanic and a woman. Hiding how afraid I was of ending up alone. Hiding under a blanket and watching old movies. Well, I'm done. I'm not hiding any of it anymore. And you know what? Nothing's going to hurt after this." She jerked out of his hold and started to walk toward the front door.

"You're not leaving in that."

She'd forgotten she wasn't exactly dressed. "Sure I am. I'm just going to drive straight home. Anyway, it's not your concern. Because I'm not your concern anymore."

The terror that she felt screaming through her chest was reflected on his face. Good. He should be afraid. This was the most terrifying experience of her life. She knew how horrible it was to lose a person you cared for. Knew what kind of void that left. And she knew that after years it didn't heal. She knew, too, you always felt the absence. She knew that she would always feel his. But she needed more. And she wasn't afraid to put it all on the line. Not now. Not after everything they had been through. Not after everything she had learned about herself. Chase was the one who had told her she needed more confidence.

Well, she had found it. But there was a cost.

Or maybe this was just the cost of loving. Of caring,

deeply and with everything she had, for the first time in so many years.

She strode across the property, not caring that she was wearing nothing more than his T-shirt, rage pouring through her. And when she arrived back at the shop she grabbed her purse and her keys, making her way to the truck. When she got there, Chase was standing against the driver's-side door. "Don't leave like this."

"Do you love me yet?"

He looked stricken. "What do you want me to say?"

"You know what I want you to say."

"You want me to lie?"

She felt like he had taken a knife and stabbed her directly through the heart. She could barely breathe. Could barely stand straight. This was… This was her worst fear come true. To open herself up so completely, to make herself so entirely vulnerable and to have it all thrown back in her face.

But in that moment, she recognized that she was untouchable from here on out. Because there was nothing that could ever, ever come close to this pain. Nothing that could ever come close to this risk.

How had she missed this before? How had she missed that failure could be such a beautiful, terrible, freeing experience?

It was the worst. Absolutely the worst. But it also broke chains that had been binding her for years. Because if someone had asked her what she was so afraid of, this would have been the answer. And she was in it. Living it. Surviving it.

"I love you," she repeated. "This is your chance. Listen to me, Chase McCormack, I am giving you a chance. I'm giving you a chance to stop being so afraid. A chance to walk out of the darkness. We've walked through it together

for a long time. So I'm asking you now to walk out of it
with me. Please."

He backed away from the truck, his jaw tense, a muscle
there twitching.

"Coward," she spat as he turned and walked away
from her. Walked away from them. Walked back into the
damned darkness.

And she got in her truck and started the engine, driving
away from him, driving away from the things she wanted
most in the entire world.

She didn't cry until she got home. But then, once she
did, she was afraid she wouldn't stop.

Fourteen

She was going to lose the bet. That was the safest thought in Anna's head as she stood in her bedroom the night of the charity event staring at the dress that was laid across her bed.

She was going to have to go there by herself. And thanks to the elaborate community theater production of their relationship everyone would know that they had broken up, since Chase wouldn't be with her. She almost laughed.

She was facing her fears all over the place, whether she wanted to or not.

Facing fears and making choices.

She wasn't going to be with Chase at the gala tonight. Wasn't going to win her money. But she had bought an incredibly slinky dress, and some more makeup. Including red lipstick. She had done all of that for him. Though in many ways it was for her, too. She had wanted that experience. To go, to prove that she was grown-up. To prove that she had transcended her upbringing and all of that.

She frowned. Was she really considering dressing differently just because she wasn't going to be with Chase?

Screw that. He might have filleted her heart and cooked it like those hideous charred Brussels sprouts cafés tries to pass off as a fancy appetizer, but he *wasn't* going to take his lessons from her. She had learned confidence. She had learned that she was stronger than she thought. She had learned that she was beautiful. And how to care. Like everything inside her had been opened up, for better or for worse. But she would never go back. No matter how bad it hurt, she wouldn't go back.

So she wouldn't go back now, either.

As she slipped the black dress over her curves, laboring over the makeup on her face and experimenting with the hairstyle she had seen online, she could only think how much harder it was to care about things. All of these things. It had been so much easier to embrace little pieces of herself. To play the part of another son for her father and throw herself into activities that made him proud, ignoring her femininity so that she never made him uncomfortable.

All of these moments of effort came at a cost. Each minute invested revealing more and more of her needs. To be seen. To be approved of.

But there were so many other reasons she had avoided this. Because this—she couldn't help but think as she looked in the mirror—looked a lot like trying. It looked a lot like caring. That was scary. It was hard.

Being rejected when you had given your best effort was so much worse than being rejected when you hadn't tried at all.

This whole being-a-woman thing—a whole woman who wanted to be with a man, who loved a man—it was hard. And it hurt.

She looked at her reflection, her eyes widening. Thanks to the smoky eye shadow her green eyes glowed, her lips looking extra pouty with the dark red color on them. She looked like one of the old screen legends she loved so much. Very Elizabeth Taylor, really.

This was her best effort. And yes, it was only a dress, and this was just looks, but it was symbolic.

She was going to lay it all on the line, and maybe people would laugh. Because the tractor mechanic in a ball gown was too ridiculous for words. But she would take the risk. And she would take it alone.

She picked up the little clutch purse that was sitting on her table. The kind of purse she'd always thought was impractical, because who wanted a bag you had to hold in your hand all night? But the salesperson at the department store had told her it went with her dress, and that altogether she looked flawless, and Anna had been in desperate need of flattery. So here she was with a clutch.

It *was* impractical. But she *did* look great.

Of course, Chase wouldn't be there to see it. She felt her eyes starting to fill with tears and she blinked, doing her best to hold it all back. She was not going to smear her makeup. She had already put it all out there for him. She would be damned if she undid all this hard work for him, too.

With that in mind, Anna got into her truck and drove herself to the ball.

"Hey, jackass," Sam shouted from across the shop. "Are you going to finish with work anytime today?"

Okay, so maybe Chase had thrown himself into work with a little more vehemence than was strictly necessary since Anna had walked out of his life.

Anna. Anna had walked out of his life. Over something as stupid as love.

If love was so stupid, it wouldn't make your insides tremble like you were staring down a black bear.

He ignored his snarky internal monologue. He had been

doing a lot of that lately. So many arguments with himself as he pounded iron at the forge. That was, when he wasn't arguing with Sam. Who was getting a little bit tired of him, all things considered.

"Do I look like I'm finished?" he shouted back.

"It's nine o'clock at night."

"That's amazing. When did you learn to tell time?"

"I counted on my fingers," Sam said, wandering deeper into the room. "So, are we just going to pretend that Anna didn't run out of your house wearing only a T-shirt the other morning?"

"I'm going to pretend that my older brother doesn't Peeping Tom everything that happens in my house."

"We live on the same property. It's bound to happen. I was on my way here when I saw her leaving. And you chasing after her. So I'm assuming you did the stupid thing."

"I told her that I couldn't be in a relationship with her." That was a lie. He had done so much more than that. He had torn both of their hearts out and stomped them into the ground. Because Sam was right, he was an idiot. But he had made a concerted effort to be a safe idiot.

How's that working for you?

"Right. Why exactly?"

"Look, the sage hermit thing is a little bit tired. You don't have a social life, I don't see you with a wife and children, so maybe you don't hang out and lecture me."

"Isn't tonight that thing?" Sam seemed undeterred by Chase's rudeness.

"What thing?"

"The charity thing that you were so intent on using to get investors. Because the two of us growing our family business and restoring the former glory of our hallowed ancestors is so important to you. And exploiting my artistic ability for your financial gain."

"Change of plans." He grunted, moving a big slab of iron

that would eventually be a gate to the side. "I'm just going to keep working. We'll figure this out without schmoozing."

"Who are you and what have you done with my brother?"

"Just shut up. If you can't do anything other than stand there looking vaguely amused at the fact that I'm going through a personal crisis, then you can go straight to hell without passing Go or collecting two hundred dollars."

"I'm not going to be able to afford Park Place anyway, because you aren't out there getting new investors."

"I'm serious, Sam," Chase shouted, throwing his hammer down on the ground. "It's all fine for you because you hold everyone at a distance."

Sam laughed. The bastard. "*I* hold everyone at a distance. What do you think you do? What do you think your endless string of one-night stands is?"

"You think I don't know? You think I don't know that it's an easy way to get some without ever having to have a conversation? I'm well aware. But I don't need you standing over there so entertained by the fact that…"

"That you actually got your heart broken?"

Chase didn't have anything to say to that. Every single word in his head evaporated like water against molten metal. He had nothing to say to that because his heart was broken. But Anna wasn't responsible. It was his own fault.

And the only reason his heart was broken was because he…

"Do you know what I said to Dad the day that he died?" Sam froze. "No."

No, he didn't. Because they had never talked about it. "The last thing I ever said to him was that I couldn't wait to get away from here. I told him I wasn't going to pound iron for the rest of my life. I was going to get away and go to college. Make something real out of myself. Like this wasn't real."

"I didn't realize."

"No. Because I didn't tell you. Because I never told anybody. But that's why I needed to fix this. It's why I wanted to expand this place."

"So it isn't really to harness my incredible talent?"

"I don't even know what it's for anymore. To what? To make up for what I said to a dead man. And for promises that I made at his grave… He can't hear me. That's the worst thing."

Sam stuffed his hands in his pockets. "Is that the only reason you're still here?"

"No. I love it here. I really do. I had to get older. I had to put some of my own sweat into this place. But now…I get it. I do. And I care about it because I care about it, not just because they cared about it. Not just because it's a legacy, but because it's worth saving. But…"

"I still remember that day. I mean, I don't just remember it," Sam said, "it's like it just happened yesterday. That feeling… The whole world changing. Everything falling right down around us. That's as strong in my head now as it was then."

"How many times can you lose everything?" Chase asked, making eye contact with his brother. "Anna is everything. Or she could be. It was easy when she was just a friend. But…I saw her in my house the other morning cooking me breakfast, wearing my T-shirt. For a second she made me feel like…like that house was our house, and she could be my…my everything."

"I wouldn't even know what that looked like for me, Chase. If you find that…grab it."

"And if I lose it?"

"You'll have no one to blame but yourself."

Chase thought back to the day his parents died. That was a kind of pain he hadn't even known existed. But, as guilty as he had felt, as many promises as he had made at his father's grave site, he couldn't blame himself for their death. It had been an accident. That was the simple truth.

But if he lost Anna now… Pushing her away hadn't been an accident. It was in his control. Fully and absolutely. And if he lost her, then it was on him.

He thought of her face as she had turned away from him, as she had gotten into her truck.

She had trusted him. His prickly Anna had trusted him with her feelings. Her vulnerability. A gift that he had never known her to give to anybody. And he had rejected it. He was no better than he had been as an angry sixteen-year-old, hurtling around the curves of the road that had destroyed his family, daring it to take him, too.

Anna, who had already endured the rejection of a mother, the silent rejection of who she was from her father, had dared to look him in the face and risk his rejection, too.

"I'll do it," Sam said, his voice rough.

"What?"

"I'm going to start…pursuing the art thing to a greater degree. I want to help. You missed this party tonight and I know it mattered to you…"

"But you hate change," Chase reminded him.

"Yeah," Sam said. "But I hate a lot of things. I have to do them anyway."

"We're still going to have to meet with investors."

"Yeah," Sam replied, stuffing his hands in his pockets. "I can help with that. You're right. This is why you're the brains and I'm the talent."

"You're a glorified blacksmith, Sam," Chase said, trying to keep the tone light because if he went too deep now he might just fall apart.

"With talent. Beyond measure," Sam said. "At least my brother has been telling me that for years."

"Your brother is smart." Though he currently felt anything but.

Sam shrugged. "Eh. Sometimes." He cleared his throat. "You discovered you cared about this place too late to ever let Dad know. That's sad. But at least Dad knew you cared about him. You know he never doubted that," Sam said. "But, damn, bro, don't leave it too late to let Anna know you care about her."

Chase looked at his brother, who was usually more cynical than he was wise, and couldn't ignore the truth ringing in his words.

Anna was the best he'd ever had. And had been for the past fifteen years of his life. Losing her…well, that was just a stupid thing to allow.

But the thing that scared him most right now was that it might already be too late. That he might have broken things beyond repair.

"And if it is too late?" he asked.

"Chase, you of all people know that when something is forged in fire it comes out the other side that much stronger." His brother's expression was hard, his dark eyes dead serious. "This is your fire. You're in it now. If you let it cool, you lose your chance. So I suggest you get your ass to wherever Anna is right now and you work at fixing this. It's either that or spend your life as a cold, useless hunk of metal that never became a damn thing."

It had not gone as badly as she'd feared. It hadn't gone perfectly, of course, but she had survived. The lowest point had been when Wendy Maxwell, who was still angry with Anna over the whole Chase thing, had wandered over to her and made disparaging comments about last season's colors and cuts, all the while implying that Anna's dress was somehow below the height of fashion. Which, whatever. She had gotten the dress on clearance, so it probably was. Anna might care about looking nice, but she didn't give a rat's ass about fashion.

She gave a couple of rat's asses about what had happened next.

Where's Chase?

Her newfound commitment to honesty and emotions had compelled her to answer honestly.

We broke up. I'm pretty upset about it.

The other woman had been in no way sympathetic and had in fact proceeded to smug all over the rest of the conversation. But she wasn't going to focus on the low.

The highs had included talking to several people whom she was going to be working with in the future. And getting two different phone numbers. She had made conversation. She had felt…like she belonged. And she didn't really think it had anything to do with the dress. Just with her. When you had already put everything out there and had it rejected, what was there to fear beyond that?

She sighed as she pulled into her driveway, straightening when she saw that there was a truck already there.

Chase's truck.

She put her own into Park, killing the engine and getting out. "What are you doing here, McCormack?" She was furious now. She was all dressed up, wearing her gorgeous dress, and she had just weathered that party on her own, and now he was here. She was going to punch his face.

Chase was sitting on her porch, wearing well-worn jeans and a tight black T-shirt, his cowboy hat firmly in place. He stood up, and as he began to walk toward her, Anna felt a raindrop fall from the sky. Because of course. He was here to kick her while she was down, almost certainly, and it was going to rain.

Thanks, Oregon.

"I came to see you." He stopped, looking her over, his jaw slightly slack. "I'm really glad that I did."

"Stop checking me out. You don't get to look at me like that. I did not put this dress on for you."

"I know."

"No, you don't know. I put this dress on for me. Because I wanted to look beautiful. Because I didn't care if anybody thought I was pretty enough, or if I'm not fashionable enough for Wendy the mule-faced ex-cheerleader. I did it because I cared. I do that now. I care. For me. Not for you."

She started to storm past him, the raindrops beginning to fall harder, thicker. He grabbed her arm and stopped her, twirling her toward him. "Don't walk away. Please."

"Give me a reason to stop walking."

"I've been doing a lot of thinking. And hammering."

"Real hammering, or is this some kind of a euphemism to let me know you're lonely?"

"Actual hammering. I didn't feel like I deserved anything else. Not after what happened."

"You don't. You don't deserve to masturbate ever again."

"Anna…"

"No," she said. "I can't do this. I can't just have a little taste of you. Not when I know what we can have. We can be everything. At first it was like you were my friend, but also we were sleeping together. And I looked at you as two different men. Chase, my friend. And Chase, the guy who was really good with his hands. And his mouth, and his tongue. You get the idea." She swallowed hard, her throat getting tight. "But at some point…it all blended together. And I can't separate it anymore. I just can't. I can't pull the love that I feel for you out of my chest and keep the friendship. Because they're all wrapped up in each other. And they've become the same thing."

"It's all or nothing," he said, his voice rough.

"Exactly."

He sighed heavily. "That's what I was afraid of."

"I'm sorry if you came over for a musical and a look at my porcupine pajamas. But I can't do it."

He tightened his hold on her, pulling her closer. "I knew it was going to be all or nothing."

"I can even understand why you think that might not be fair—"

"No. When you told me you loved me, I knew it was everything. Or nothing. That was what scared me so much. I have known… For a lot of years, I've realized that you were one of the main supports of my entire life. I knew you were one of the things that kept me together after my parents died. One of the only things. And I knew that if I ever lost you…it might finish me off completely."

"I'm sorry. But I can't live my life as your support."

"I know. I'm not suggesting that you do. It's just…when we started sleeping together, I had the same realization. That we weren't going to be able to separate the physical from the emotional, from our friendship. That it wasn't as simple as we pretended it could be. When I came downstairs and saw you in my kitchen…I saw the potential for something I never thought I could have."

"Why didn't you think you could have that?"

"I was too afraid. Tragedy happens to other people, Anna. Until it happens to you. And then it's like…the safety net is just gone. And everything you never thought you could be touched by is suddenly around every corner. You realize you aren't special. You aren't safe. If I could lose both my parents like that…I could lose anybody."

"You can't live that way," she said, her heart crumpling. "How in the world can you live that way?"

"You live halfway," he said. "You let yourself have a little bit of things, and not all of them. You pour your commitment into a place. Your passion into a job, into a goal of restoring a family name when your family is already gone. So you can't disappoint them even if you do fail." He took a deep breath. "You keep the best woman you know as a friend, because if she ever became more, your feelings for her could consume you. Anna… If I lost you…I would lose everything."

She could only stand there, looking at him, feeling like the earth was breaking to pieces beneath her feet. "Why did you—"

"I wanted to at least see it coming." He lowered his head, shaking it slowly. "I was such an idiot. For a long time. And afraid. I think it's impossible to go through tragedy like I did, like we did, and not have it change you. I'm not sure it's even possible to escape it doing so much as defining you. But you can choose how. It was so easy for me to see how you protected yourself. How you shielded yourself. But I didn't see that I was doing the same thing."

"I didn't know," she said, feeling stupid. Feeling blind.

"Because I didn't tell you." He reached up, drawing his thumb over her cheekbone, his expression so empty, so sad. Another side of Chase she hadn't seen very often. But it was there. It had always been there, she realized that now. "But I'm telling you now. I'm scared. I've been scared for a long time. And I've made a lot of promises to ghosts to try to atone for stupid things I said when my parents were alive. But I've been too afraid to make promises to the people that are actually still in my life. Too afraid to love the people that are still here. It's easier to make promises to ghosts, Anna. I'm done with that.

"You are here," he said, cupping her face now, holding her steady. "You're with me. And I can have you as long as I'm not too big an idiot. As long as you still want to have me. You put yourself out there for me, and I rejected you. I'm so sorry. I know what that cost you, Anna, because I know you. And please understand I didn't reject you because it wasn't enough. Because you weren't enough. It's because you were too much, and I wasn't enough. But I'm going to do my best to be enough for you now. Now and forever."

She could hardly believe what she was hearing, could hardly believe that Chase was standing there making declarations to her. The kind that sounded an awful lot like love. The kind that sounded an awful lot like exactly what she wanted to hear. "Is this because I'm wearing a dress?"

"No." He chuckled. "You could be wearing coveralls. You could be wearing nothing. Actually, I think I like you best in nothing. But whatever you're wearing, it wouldn't change this. It wouldn't change how I feel. Because I love you in every possible way. As my friend, as my lover. I love you in whatever you wear, a ball gown or engine grease. I love you working on tractors and trying to explain to me how an engine works and watching musicals."

"But do you love my porcupine pajamas?" she asked, her voice breaking.

"I'm pretty ambivalent about your porcupine pajamas, I'm not going to lie. But if they're a nonnegotiable part of the deal, then I can adjust."

She shook her head. "They aren't nonnegotiable. But I probably will irritate you with them." Then she sobbed, unable to hold her emotions back any longer. She wrapped her arms around his neck, burying her face in his skin, breathing his scent in. "Chase, I love you so much. Look what we were protecting ourselves from."

He laughed. "When you put it that way, it seems like we were being pretty stupid."

"Fear is stupid. And it's strong."

He tightened his hold on her. "It isn't stronger than this."

Not stronger than fifteen years of friendship, than holding each other through grief and pleasure, laughter and pain.

When she had pulled up and seen his truck here, Anna Brown had murder on her mind. And now, everything was different.

"Remember when you promised you were going to make me a woman?" she asked.

"Right. I do. You laughed at me."

"Yes, I did." She stretched up on her toes and kissed his lips. "Chase McCormack, I'm pretty sure you did make me a woman. Maybe not in the way you meant. But you made me feel…like a whole person. Like I could finally put together all the parts of me and just be me. Not hide any of it anymore."

He closed his eyes, pressing his forehead against hers. "I'm glad, Anna. Because you sure as hell made me a man. The man that I want to be, the man that I need to be. I can't change the past, and I can't live in it anymore, either."

"Good. Then I think we should go ahead and make ourselves a future."

"Works for me." He smiled. "I love you. You're everything."

"I love you, too." It felt so good to say that. To say it and not be afraid. To show her whole heart and not hold anything back.

"I bet that I can make you say you love me at least a hundred more times tonight. I bet I can get you to say it every day for the rest of our lives."

She smiled, taking his hand and walking toward the house, not caring about the rain. "I bet you can."

He led her inside, leaving a trail of clothes in the hall behind them, leaving her beautiful dress on the floor. She didn't care at all.

"And I bet—" he wrapped his arm around her waist, then laid her down on the bed "—tonight I can make you scream."

"I'll take that bet," she said, wrapping her legs around his hips.

And that was a bet they both won.

* * * * *

Meet all the cowboys in Copper Ridge!

SHOULDA BEEN A COWBOY
PART TIME COWBOY
BROKEDOWN COWBOY
BAD NEWS COWBOY
A COPPER RIDGE CHRISTMAS
TAKE ME, COWBOY
ONE NIGHT CHARMER

and

TOUGH LUCK HERO
Available July 2016

LAST CHANCE REBEL
Available September 2016

HOLD ME, COWBOY
Available November 2016

If you can't get enough Maisey Yates,
try her bestselling books from Harlequin Presents!

MARRIED FOR AMARI'S HEIR,
part of the
ONE NIGHT WITH CONSEQUENCES *series*
Available now!

* * *

If you fell for Ace the bartender's charm, don't miss
the next COPPER RIDGE *novel,*
ONE NIGHT CHARMER,
from USA TODAY *bestselling author Maisey Yates*
and HQN Books!

*Read on for an exclusive sneak preview...
Copper Ridge, Oregon's favorite bachelor is about
to meet his match!*

*If the devil wore flannel, he'd look like Ace Thompson.
He's gruff. Opinionated. Infernally hot. The last person
Sierra West wants to ask for a bartending job—not that
she has a choice. Ever since discovering that her
"perfect" family is built on a lie, Sierra has been
determined to make it on her own. Resisting her new
boss should be easy when they're always bickering.
Until one night, the squabbling stops...and something
far more dangerous takes over.
Ace has a personal policy against messing around with
staff—or with spoiled rich girls. But there's a steel
backbone beneath Sierra's silver-spoon upbringing.
She's tougher than he thought, and so much more
tempting. Enough to make him want to break all his
rules, even if it means risking his heart...*

*Read on for this special extended excerpt from
ONE NIGHT CHARMER
by* USA TODAY *bestselling author Maisey Yates.*

CHAPTER ONE

THERE WERE TWO PEOPLE in Copper Ridge, Oregon, who—between them—knew nearly every secret of every person in town. The first was Pastor John Thompson, who heard confessions of sin and listened to people pour out their hearts when they were going through trials and tribulations.

The second was Ace Thompson, owner of the most popular bar in town, son of the pastor and probably the least likely to attend church on Sunday or any other day.

There was no question that his father knew a lot of secrets, though Ace was pretty certain he himself got the more honest version. His father spent time standing behind the pulpit; Ace stood behind a bar. And there he learned the deepest and darkest situations happening in the lives of other townspeople while never revealing any of his own. He supposed, pastor or bartender, that was kind of the perk.

They poured it all out for you, and you got to keep your secrets bottled up inside.

That was how Ace liked it. Every night of the week, he had the best seat in the house for whatever show Copper Ridge wanted to put on. And he didn't even have to pay for it.

And with his newest acquisition, the show was about to get a whole lot better.

"Really?" Jack Monaghan sat down at the bar, beer in hand, his arm around his new fiancée, Kate Garrett. "A mechanical bull?"

"That's right, Monaghan. This is a classy establishment, after all."

"Seriously," Connor Garrett said, taking the seat next to Jack, followed by his wife, Liss. "Where did you get that thing?"

"I traded it. Guy down in Tolowa owed me some money and he didn't have it. So he said I could come by and look at his stash of trash. Lo and behold, I discovered Ferdinand over there."

"Congratulations," Kate said. "I didn't think anything could make this place more of a dive. I was wrong."

"You're a peach, Kate," Ace said.

The woman smiled broadly and wrapped her arm around Jack's, leaning in and resting her cheek on his shoulder.

"Can we get a round?" Connor asked.

Ace continued to listen to their conversation as he served up their usual brew, enjoying the happy tenor of the conversation, since the downers would probably be around later to dish out woe while he served up harder liquor. The Garretts were good people, he mused. Always had been. Both before he'd left Copper Ridge, and since he'd come back.

His focus was momentarily pulled away when the pretty blonde who'd been hanging out in the dining room all evening drinking with friends approached the aforementioned Ferdinand.

He hadn't had too many people ride the bull yet, and he had to admit, he was finding it a pretty damn enjoyable novelty.

The woman tossed her head, her tan cowboy hat staying in place while her blond curls went wild around her shoulders. She wrapped her hands around the harness on top of the mechanical creature and hoisted herself up. Her movements were unsteady, and he had a feeling, based on the amount of time the group had been here, and how often the men in the group had come and gone from the bar, that she was more than a little bit tipsy.

Best seat in the house. He always had the best seat in the house.

She glanced up as she situated herself and he got a good look at her face. There was a determined glint in her eyes, her brows locked together, her lips pursed into a tight circle. She wasn't just tipsy, she was pissed. Looking down at the bull like it was her own personal Everest and she was determined to conquer it along with her rage. He wondered what a bedazzled little thing like her had to be angry about. A broken nail, maybe. A pair of shoes that she really wanted that was unavailable in her size.

She nodded once, her expression growing even *more* determined as she signaled the employee Ace had operating the controls tonight.

Ace moved nearer to the bar, planting his hands flat on the surface. "This probably won't end well."

The patrons at the bar turned their heads toward the scene. And he noticed Jack's posture go rigid. "Is that—"

"Yes," Kate said.

The mechanical bull pitched forward and the petite blonde sitting on top of it pitched right along with it. She managed to stay seated, but in Ace's opinion that was a miracle. The bull went back again, and the woman straightened, arching her back and thrusting her breasts forward, her head tilted upward, the overhead lighting bathing her pretty face in a golden glow. And for a moment, just a moment, she looked like a graceful, dirty angel getting into the rhythm of the kind of riding Ace preferred above anything else.

Then the great automated beast pitched forward again and the little lady went over the top, down onto the mats underneath. There were howls from her so-called friends as they enjoyed her deposition just a little too much.

She stood on shaky legs and walked back over to the group, picking up a shot glass and tossing back another, her face twisted into an expression that suggested this was not typical behavior for her.

Kate frowned and got up from her stool, making her way over to the other woman.

Ace had a feeling he should know the woman's name, had a feeling that he probably did somewhere in the back corner of his mind. He knew everyone. Which meant that he knew a lot *about* a lot of people, recognized nearly every face he passed on the street. He could usually place them with their most defining life moments, as those were the things that often spilled out on the bar top after a few shots too many.

But it didn't mean he could put a name to every face. There were simply too many of them.

"Who is that?" he asked.

"Sierra West," Jack said, something strange in his tone.

"Oh, right."

He knew the West family well enough, or rather, he knew of them. Everyone did. Though they were hardly the type to frequent his establishment. Sierra did, which would explain why she was familiar, though they never made much in the way of conversation. She was the type who was always absorbed in her friends or her cell phone when she came to place her order. No deep confessionals from Sierra over drinks.

He'd always found it a little strange she patronized his bar when the rest of the West family didn't.

Dive bars weren't really their thing.

He imagined mechanical bulls probably weren't, either. Judging not just on Sierra's pedigree, but on the poor performance.

"No cotillions going on tonight, I guess," Ace said.

Jack turned his head sharply, his expression dark. "What's that supposed to mean?"

"Nothing."

He didn't know why, but his statement had clearly offended Monaghan. Ace wasn't in the business of voicing his opinion. He was in the business of listening. Listening and serving. No one needed to know his take on a damn thing. They just wanted a sounding board to voice their own opinions and hear them echoed back.

Typically, he had no trouble with that. This had been a little slipup.

"She's not so bad," Jack said.

Sierra was a friend of Jack's fiancée, that much was obvious. Kate was over there talking to her, expression concerned. Sierra still looked mutinous. Ace was starting to wonder if she was mad at the entire world, or if something in particular had set her off.

"I'm sure she isn't." He wasn't sure of any such thing. In fact, if he knew one thing about the world and all the people in it, it was that there was a particular type who used their every advantage in life to take whatever they wanted, whenever they wanted it, regardless of promises made. Whether they were words whispered in the dark or vows spoken in front of whole crowds of loved ones.

He was a betting man. And he would lay odds that Sierra West was one of those people. She was the type. Rich, a big fish in the small pond of the community and beautiful. That combination pretty much guaranteed her whatever she wanted. And when the option for *whatever you wanted* was available, very few people resisted it.

Hell, why would you? There were a host of things he would change if he had infinite money and power.

But just because he figured he'd be in the same boat if he were rich and almighty didn't mean he had to like it on others.

HE LOOKED BACK over at Kate, who patted her friend on the shoulder before shaking her head and walking back toward the group. "She didn't want to come sit with us or anything," Kate said, looking frustrated.

The Garrett-Monaghan crew lingered at the bar for another couple of hours before they were replaced by another set of customers. Sierra's group thinned out a little bit, but didn't disperse completely. A couple of the guys were starting to get rowdy, and Ace was starting to think he was going to have to play the part of his own bouncer tonight. It wouldn't be the first time.

Fortunately, the noisier members of the group slowly trickled outside. He watched as Sierra got up and made her way back to the bathroom, leaving a couple of girls—one of whom he assumed was the designated driver—sitting at the table.

The tab was caught up, so he didn't really care how it all went down. He wasn't a babysitter, after all.

He turned, grabbed a rag out of the bucket beneath the counter and started to wipe it down. When he looked up again, the girls who had been sitting at the table were gone, and Sierra West was standing in the center of the room looking around like she was lost.

Then she glanced his way, and her eyes lit up like a sinner looking at salvation.

Wrong guess, honey.

She wandered over to the bar, her feet unsteady. "Did you see where my friends went?"

She had that look about her. Like a lost baby deer. All wide, dewy eyes and unsteady limbs. And damned if she wasn't cute as hell.

"Out the door," he said, almost feeling sorry for her. Almost.

She wasn't the first pretty young drunk to get ditched in his bar by stupid friends. She was also exactly the kind of woman he avoided at all costs, no matter how cute or seemingly vulnerable she was.

"What?" She swayed slightly. "They weren't supposed to leave me."

She sounded mystified. Completely dumbfounded that anyone would ever leave her high and dry.

"I figured," he said. "Here's a tip—get better friends."

She frowned. "They're the best friends I have."

He snorted. "That's a sad story."

She held up her hand, the broad gesture out of place coming from such a refined creature. "Just a second."

"Sure."

She turned away, heading toward the door and out to the parking lot.

He swore. He didn't know if she had a car out there, but she was way too skunked to drive.

"Watch the place, Jenna," he said to one of the waitresses, who nodded and assumed a rather important-looking position with her hands flat on the bar and a rag in her hand, as though she were ready to wipe crumbs away with serious authority.

He rounded the counter and followed the same path Sierra had just taken out into the parking lot. He looked around for a moment and didn't see her. Then he looked down and there she was, sitting on the edge of the curb. "Everything okay?"

That was a stupid question; he already knew the answer. She looked up. "No."

He let out a long-drawn-out sigh. The problem was, he'd followed her out here. If he had just let her walk out the door, then nothing but the pine trees and the seagulls would have been responsible for her. But no, he'd had to follow. He'd been concerned about her driving. And now he would have to follow through on that concern.

"You don't have a ride?"

She shook her head, looking miserable. "Everyone left me. Because they aren't nice. You're right. I do need better friends."

"Yes," he said, "you do. And let me go ahead and tell you right now, I won't be one of them. But as long as you don't live somewhere ridiculous like Portland, I can give you a ride home."

And this, right here, was the curse of owning a bar. Whether he should or not, he felt responsible in these situations. She was compromised, it was late, and she was alone. He could not let her meander her way back home. Not when he could easily see that she got there safely.

"A ride?" She frowned, her delicate features lit dramatically by the security light hanging on the front of the bar.

"I know your daddy probably told you not to take rides from strangers, but trust me, I'm the safest bet around. Unless you want to call someone." He checked his watch. "It's inching close to last call. I'm betting not very many people are going to come out right now."

She shook her head slowly. "Probably not."

He sighed heavily, reaching into his pocket and wrapping his fingers around his keys. "All right, come on. Get in the truck."

Sierra looked up at her unlikely, bearded, plaid-clad savior. She knew who he was, of course. Ace Thompson was the owner of the bar, and she bought beer from him at least twice a month when she came out with her friends. They'd exchanged money and drinks across the counter more times than she could recall, but this was more words than she'd ever exchanged with him in her life.

She was angry at herself. For getting drunk. For going out with the biggest jerks in the local rodeo club. For getting on the back of a mechanical bull and opening herself up to their derision—because honestly, when you put your drunk self up on a fake, bucking animal, you pretty much deserved it. And most of all, for sitting down in the parking lot acting like she was going to cry just because she had been ditched by said jerky friends.

Oh, and being *caught* at what was most definitely an epic low made it all even worse. He'd almost certainly seen her inglorious dismount off the mechanical bull, then witnessed everyone leaving without her.

She'd been so sure today couldn't get any worse.

She'd been wrong.

"I'm fine," she said, and she could have bitten off her own tongue, because she wasn't fine. As much as she wanted to pretend she didn't need his help, she kind of did. Granted, she could call Colton or Madison. But if her sister had to drive all the way down to town from the family estate she would probably kill Sierra. And if she called Colton's house his fiancée would probably kill Sierra.

Either way, that made for a dead Sierra.

She wasn't speaking to her father. Which, really, was the root of today's evil.

"Sure you are. *Most* girls who end up sitting on their behinds at 1:00 a.m. in a parking lot are just fine."

She blinked, trying to bring his face into focus. He refused to be anything but a fuzzy blur. "I am."

For some reason, her stubbornness was on full display, and most definitely outweighed her common sense. That was probably related to the alcohol. And to the fact that all of her restraint had been torn down hours ago. Sometime early this morning when she had screamed at her father and told him she never wanted to see him again, because she'd found out he was a liar. A cheater.

Right, so that was probably why she was feeling rebellious. Angry in general. But she probably shouldn't direct it at the person who was offering a helping hand.

"Don't make me ask you twice, Sierra. It's going to

make me get real grumpy, and I don't think you'll like that." Ace shifted his stance, crossing his arms over his broad chest—she was pretty sure it was broad, either that or she was seeing double—and looked down at her.

She got to her wobbly feet, pitching slightly to the side before steadying herself. Her head was spinning, her stomach churning, and she was just mad. Because she felt like crap. Because she knew better than to drink like this, at least when she wasn't in the privacy of her own home.

"Which truck?" she asked, rubbing her forehead.

He turned, not waiting for her, and began to walk across the parking lot. She followed as quickly as she could. Fortunately, the lot was mostly empty, so she didn't have to watch much but the back of Ace as they made their way to the vehicle. It wasn't a new, flashy truck. It was old, but it was in good condition. Better than most she'd seen at such an advanced age. But then, Ace wasn't a rancher. He owned a bar, so it wasn't like his truck saw all that much action.

She stood in front of the passenger-side door for a long moment before realizing he was not coming around to open it for her. Her face heated as she jerked open the door for herself and climbed up inside.

It had a bench seat. And she found herself clinging to the door, doing her best to keep the expansive seat between them as wide as possible. She was suddenly conscious of the fact that he was a very large man. Tall, broad, muscular. She'd known that, somewhere in the back of her mind. But the way he filled up the cab of a truck containing just the two of them was much more significant than the way he filled the space in a vast and crowded bar.

He started the engine, saying nothing as he put the truck in Reverse and began to pull out of the lot. She looked straight ahead, desperate to find something to say. The silence was oppressive, heavy around them. It made her feel twitchy, nervous. She always knew what to say. She was in command of every social situation she stepped into. People found her charming, and if they didn't, they never said otherwise. Because she was Sierra West, and her family name carried with it the burden of mandatory respect from the people of Copper Ridge.

She took a deep breath, trying to ease the pressure in her chest, trying to remove the weight that was sitting there.

"What's your sign?" Somehow, her fuzzy brain had retrieved that as a conversation starter. The moment the words left her mouth she wanted to stuff them back in and swallow them.

To her surprise, he laughed. "Caution."

"What?"

"I'm a caution sign, baby. And it would be in your best interest to obey the warning…"

Don't miss what happens when Sierra doesn't heed his advice in
ONE NIGHT CHARMER
by USA TODAY bestselling author Maisey Yates!

COMING NEXT MONTH FROM

HARLEQUIN

Desire

Available May 10, 2016

#2443 TWINS FOR THE TEXAN
Billionaires and Babies • by Charlene Sands
When Brooke McKay becomes pregnant after a one-night stand with a sexy rancher, she tracks him down to discover he's a widower struggling with toddler twins! Can she help as his nanny before falling in love—and delivering her baby bombshell?

#2444 IN PURSUIT OF HIS WIFE
Texas Cattleman's Club: Lies and Lullabies
by Kristi Gold
A British billionaire and his convenient wife wed for all the wrong reasons...and she can't stay when he won't open his heart, even though their desire is undeniable. But now that she's pregnant, the stakes for their reunion are even higher...

#2445 SECRET BABY SCANDAL
Bayou Billionaires • by Joanne Rock
Wealthy football star Jean-Pierre despises the media. When rumors fly, he knows who to blame—the woman who's avoided him since their red-hot night together. His proposition: pretend they're a couple to end the scandal. But Tatiana has secrets of her own...

#2446 THE CEO'S LITTLE SURPRISE
Love and Lipstick • by Kat Cantrell
CEO Gage Branson isn't above seducing his ex, rival CEO Cassandra Clare, for business, but when he's accused of the corporate espionage threatening Cassie's company, it gets personal fast. And then he finds out someone's been hiding a little secret...

#2447 FROM FRIEND TO FAKE FIANCÉ
Mafia Moguls • by Jules Bennett
Mobster Mac O'Shea is more than willing to play fiancé with his sexy best friend at a family wedding. But it doesn't take long for Mac to realize the heat between them is all too real...

#2448 HIS SEDUCTION GAME PLAN
Sons of Privilege • by Katherine Garbera
Ferrin is the only one who can clear Hunter's name, and Hunter isn't above using charm to persuade her. He says he's only interested in the secrets she protects—so why can't he get his enemy's daughter out of his mind?

REQUEST YOUR FREE BOOKS!
2 FREE NOVELS PLUS 2 FREE GIFTS!

ⓗ HARLEQUIN®

Desire

ALWAYS POWERFUL, PASSIONATE AND PROVOCATIVE

YES! Please send me 2 FREE Harlequin® Desire novels and my 2 FREE gifts (gifts are worth about $10). After receiving them, if I don't wish to receive any more books, I can return the shipping statement marked "cancel." If I don't cancel, I will receive 6 brand-new novels every month and be billed just $4.55 per book in the U.S. or $5.24 per book in Canada. That's a savings of at least 13% off the cover price! It's quite a bargain! Shipping and handling is just 50¢ per book in the U.S. and 75¢ per book in Canada.* I understand that accepting the 2 free books and gifts places me under no obligation to buy anything. I can always return a shipment and cancel at any time. Even if I never buy another book, the two free books and gifts are mine to keep forever.

225/326 HDN GH2P

Name	(PLEASE PRINT)	
Address		Apt. #
City	State/Prov.	Zip/Postal Code

Signature (if under 18, a parent or guardian must sign)

Mail to the **Reader Service:**
IN U.S.A.: P.O. Box 1867, Buffalo, NY 14240-1867
IN CANADA: P.O. Box 609, Fort Erie, Ontario L2A 5X3

Want to try two free books from another line?
Call 1-800-873-8635 or visit www.ReaderService.com.

* Terms and prices subject to change without notice. Prices do not include applicable taxes. Sales tax applicable in N.Y. Canadian residents will be charged applicable taxes. Offer not valid in Quebec. This offer is limited to one order per household. Not valid for current subscribers to Harlequin Desire books. All orders subject to credit approval. Credit or debit balances in a customer's account(s) may be offset by any other outstanding balance owed by or to the customer. Please allow 4 to 6 weeks for delivery. Offer available while quantities last.

Your Privacy—The Reader Service is committed to protecting your privacy. Our Privacy Policy is available online at www.ReaderService.com or upon request from the Reader Service.

We make a portion of our mailing list available to reputable third parties that offer products we believe may interest you. If you prefer that we not exchange your name with third parties, or if you wish to clarify or modify your communication preferences, please visit us at www.ReaderService.com/consumerschoice or write to us at Reader Service Preference Service, P.O. Box 9062, Buffalo, NY 14240-9062. Include your complete name and address.

HD15

SPECIAL EXCERPT FROM

HARLEQUIN *Desire*

*When Brooke becomes pregnant after a one-night stand
with a sexy rancher, she tracks him down to discover
he's a widower struggling with toddler twins! Can she
help as his nanny before falling in love—and delivering
her baby bombshell?*

Read on for a sneak peek of
TWINS FOR THE TEXAN
the latest book by USA TODAY *bestselling author*
Charlene Sands *in the bestselling*
BILLIONAIRES AND BABIES *series*

Grateful to have made it without getting lost, Brooke had
to contend with the fact she was *here*. And now, one way
or another, her life was going to change forever. She rang
the doorbell. A moment later, she stood face-to-face with
Wyatt.

Who was holding a squirming baby boy.

It was the last thing she expected.

"Wyatt?" She was rendered speechless, staring at the
man who'd made her insides quiver just one month ago.

"Come in, Brooke. I'm glad you made it."

She stared at him, still not believing what she was
seeing. He'd never mentioned having a child. Although,
there'd seemed to be a silent agreement between them
not to delve too deeply into their private lives.

She stepped inside and Wyatt closed the door behind
her. "This is Brett, my son. He was supposed to be

sleeping by the time you arrived. Obviously that didn't happen. Babies tend to make liars of their parents, and it's been rough without a nanny."

"He's beautiful."

"Thanks, he's the best part of me. Well, him and his twin, Brianna."

"There's two of them?"

"I want to explain. Why don't you have a seat?" He started walking and she followed. "You look pretty, by the way," he said, his cowboy charm taking hold again, and she had trouble remembering how he'd dumped her after a spectacular night of sex.

A night when they'd conceived a child.

"You didn't tell me you had children."

"I just wanted to be me—not a father, not a widower—that night. My friends are forever saying I need to find myself again. That's what I was trying to do."

She inhaled a sharp breath, everything becoming clear.

If she were brave, she'd reveal her pregnancy to Wyatt and try to cope with the decisions they would make together. But her courage failed her. How could she tell this widower with twins he was about to be a father again?

Don't miss
TWINS FOR THE TEXAN
by USA TODAY bestselling author Charlene Sands
available May 2016 wherever
Harlequin® Desire books and ebooks are sold.

www.Harlequin.com

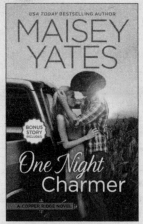

USA TODAY BESTSELLING AUTHOR

MAISEY YATES

BONUS STORY INCLUDED

One Night
Charmer

A COPPER RIDGE NOVEL

$7.99 U.S./$9.99 CAN.

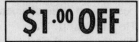